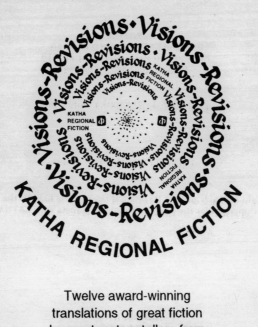

KATHA REGIONAL FICTION

Twelve award-winning
translations of great fiction
by master story tellers from
the Katha Translation Contest

Edited by
Keerti Ramachandra

KATHA

Rupa.Co

Published by
KATHA
Building Centre, Sarai Kale Khan,
Nizamuddin East, New Delhi 110013
Phone : 4628227; 4628254

First published by Katha, July 1995

Distributed by
RUPA & CO.
15, Bankim Chatterjee Street,
Calcutta 700070

94, South Malaka,
Allahabad 211001

P.G. Solanki Path,
Lamington Road,
Bombay 400007

7/16 Ansari Road,
Daryaganj,
New Delhi 110002

General Series Editor: Geeta Dharmarajan
Assistant Editor: Meenakshi Sharma
Design: Neeraj & Pallavi Sahai

Typeset in 9 on 13pt Bookman by Suresh Sharma at Katha
Printed at Gopsons Papers Pvt. Ltd, NOIDA (U.P.)

ISBN 81-85586-22-5 (hardback);   ISBN 81-85586-21-7 (paperback)

CONTENTS

INTRODUCTION

Visions-Revisions is the outcome of the first ever translation contest conducted by Katha. A contest of this magnitude, both in scope and reach, was perhaps held for the first time in the country. In an attempt to get a fair representation, Katha consciously chose three languages from each region. Aspiring translators were invited to render into English, outstanding short stories from twelve languages. And thirteen hundred persons responded.

The task of choosing the stories to be translated was daunting. The process of selecting the winners was even more so. As always, the Friends of Katha rallied round us and undertook the responsibility willingly and cheerfully. The British High Commission, British Council Division, was spontaneous in accepting our proposal to co-conduct the contest and offered assistance in terms of services and funds. The contest was followed by a workshop for the prize-winners, runners-up and invited guests. The Awards ceremony, presided over by the Vice-President, Shri K R Narayanan was the culmination of a memorable event.

The overwhelming response to the contest bore out Katha's conviction that more people are interested in translation and translating than are given credit for. It was heartening to see that the entrants came from such diverse backgrounds as nuclear medicine and apple farming, architecture and chemical engineering, classical music and civil service, with of course a fair number from the media and academics.

Translation as an attempt at revealing the author's vision in a different linguistic system and another time frame is often exasperating, frequently frustrating and almost always an incomplete effort. As Poornachandra Tejasvi, the eminent Kannada writer remarks, "Translations are successes or failures to varying degrees. They remain in a state of perpetual imperfection ..." And yet there is that moment of perfect comprehension, when a seemingly untranslatable phrase yields to the translator's perseverance and suddenly everything falls into place. The experience of having caught the author's vision and presented it as honestly as one can in a re-vision, is what makes translation a worthwhile act in itself.

Through the efforts of the award-winning translators, you have available to you twelve stories from stalwarts in the realm of short fiction in their respective languages. Every story is a nugget which explores, crystallizes and interprets a singular incident, an emotion, an attitude, a place, a character, a relationship. They differ marvellously in style and content and reveal the possibilities and achievements of this most variegated literary form.

No matter what the region or which the language, the themes are universal, the characters and situations credible. From the lyrical to the stark, the familiar and predictable to the exotic and supernatural, these stories will not leave you unaffected. Many of them, the authors confess, originated in personal experiences. Others are drawn from the writers' observations of life and people around them, while some are rooted in mythology and literature.

Given then, the vision of the author, and the re-vision of the translator, where does the editor come in? Unfortunately, there is no set code for editors. One has to go by a few thumb rules, more often inferred rather than explicitly stated. We have tried not to intrude or take over from either author or translator, and abide by those guidelines endorsed by Tejasvi, that translation should first and foremost be readable and interesting prose. Our primary concern has been to ensure a smooth transition from the author's vision through the translator's re-vision to the reader's perception.

The gestation period for this volume has been long, and fraught with anxiety, excitement, fatigue and elation for Meenakshi Sharma, who has been with the project from the start, and me.

But under the expert guidance and care of Geeta Dharmarajan, the effort was almost painless. To her, and all at Katha, thank you!

June, 1995   Keerti Ramachandra

ACKNOWLEDGEMENTS

We would like to thank:

the British High Commission, British Council Division, for their unstinting support and keen interest at every stage of the contest. In particular, we are grateful to N Gilroy-Scott, Richard Walker, K Ramanathan, Rajani Badlani, Sushma Behl and Praveen Narang

the writers who allowed us to use their stories for the contest all the friends of Katha who recommended stories and even translated them so that we could select the final twelve

our resource persons in the various languages, whose difficult task it was to shortlist the translations - Enakshi Chatterjee, JP Das, Sudhanva Deshpande, Ganesh Devy, Kasturi Kanthan, Gita Krishnankutty, Bibhu Mohanty, Balu Rao, Anisur Rehman and Nalini Taneja

the judges who gave so freely of their precious time to choose the winners – U R Anantha Murthy, Geeta Dharmarajan, N S Jagannathan, N Gilroy-Scott

Meera Warrier, Renuka Ramachandran and Tulsi Dharmarajan for initiating and seeing the contest and the workshop through

a second set of resource people who helped with the editing of the prize-winning entries - Jayeeta Sharma, Indira Mukherjee, Srijata Roy, Anjali Nayyar, Ashutosh Roy, Radha Nambiar, Vinoo Hora, Iram Sultan and Jasjit Man Singh

Bindu Nambiar and Gita Jayaraj who saw the manuscript till its final form.

We owe a debt of gratitude to Muriel Faleiro, who is no longer with us, for recommending the Konkani story and introducing the Konkani literary scene to Katha.

A COMMITMENT TO TRANSLATION

As well as the more commonplace 'process of turning from one language into another' among its many definitions of translation, the Oxford English Dictionary includes 'the removal or conveyance from one person, place or condition to another.' In this sense, translation is at the heart of all the British Council's activities not only in India but worldwide. Central to the British Council's role is a belief that cultures in contact refresh themselves and re-define one another by such exposure. It would be difficult to improve on the notion of translation as a key metaphor informing all of our work. The British Council in India aims to strengthen the Indo-British relationship to the mutual benefit and understanding of both countries and cultures. What better channel could it find to pursue this aim than through assisting Katha in its translation activities?

For the past two years we have co-organised two successful translation seminars, and with the support of the Charles Wallace India Trust have offered writing fellowships at the Universities of Kent and Stirling in Britain. Two of these fellows are actively engaged in the translation of creative works in Indian languages into English. Similarly, we have supported and organised visits to India by British specialists such as Rupert Snell and William Radice who respectively translate from Hindi and Bangla into English. At the time of writing we are also discussing the possibility of setting up a new fellowship for an Indian translator at the Centre for Translation Studies at the University of East Anglia. Our collaboration with Katha has not only been successful in helping to establish the importance of translation in India but has also brought the richness and variety of writing in Indian languages to the attention of a wider public both in India and Britain.

The British Council is proud to be associated with Katha in organising this short story translation project and publishing the twelve award-winning stories, many of which are appearing in English for the first time. Translation is arguably never fully realised since it sets itself the impossible goal of re-creating in one language what has already been best expressed in another. Nevertheless, the process and the final product of translation, when successful, can result in a new creation inspired by but not a slave to the original source. We are certain that these translations will attract a wider and well deserved attention to the work of their original authors and to that of the translators themselves.

We greatly appreciate the dedicated hard work Ms Geeta Dharmarajan and her colleagues at Katha have put into making this project a success and are delighted to reaffirm our commitment to translation - in all its senses - in India.

New Delhi
April 25, 1995

Richard Walker
First Secretary
(Cultural Affairs)
British Council Division

The Award-winning Translators

ASSAMESE
Ranjita Biswas

BANGLA
Shampa Ghosh
and
Dhritiman Chaterji

GUJARATI
Madhukar Hegde

HINDI
Premila Condillac
and
Ruth Vanita

KANNADA
Vanamala Viswanath

KONKANI
Vidya Pai

MALAYALAM
CPA Vasudevan

MARATHI
Padmaja Punde
and
Bipin Bhise

ORIYA
Maurice Shukla

PUNJABI
Jasjit Man Singh
Devinder Kaur Assa Singh

TAMIL
Shakuntala Ramani

URDU
Sara Rai

* We had joint winners in Bangla, Hindi and Marathi. Since combined translations were not feasible, one of the two prize-winning entries was selected for publication.
– Editor

translated by
Ranjita Biswas

I t was a happy day for the people of this small, almost rural town when a pump was installed to supply water to the temple. The town drew its importance from this mandir. People flocked from far and wide to pay obeisance at the shrine. By now, stories of the Devi's great power and benevolence to the worshippers had, through constant retelling, grown to the proportion of legends. No one cared whether these legends were authentic or not. What mattered was that the Devi was more than a mute piece of stone, that she was alive to their prayers. One of the bhaktas had now arranged for water to be pumped up from the pond nearby. The pump was a convenience that everyone welcomed happily.

The only exception was Hanu. He was incensed by this new device. So far it had been his duty to fetch water from the pond for the bhaktas. The cool water that

MANDIR

by Harekrishna Deka

slaked their thirst had meant a few coins in his pocket, enough for his simple needs. But then, Hanu's livelihood was less important than the convenience of hundreds of pilgrims.

Even so, Hanu could not abandon the mandir. Angry, no doubt, at his loss, he still clung to the premises. The numerous bhaktas might have been ignorant of his connection with the shrine, but the portly purohit knew all about it.

Hanu's appearance did not evoke sympathy. He was ugly. The first thing that struck one was his enormous hump. He looked as if he carried a heavy burden on his back. The protruding upper lip below a flat nose, accentuated his resemblance to simian ancestors. His very name was bequeathed to him by his ugly face, and Hanuman had been gradually shortened to Hanu.

Leprosy had made Hanu's body swell, adding to his ugliness. It had eaten away his flesh and the tips of a few fingers and toes had fallen off. Though detected recently, it had already cost him his allotted place on the verandah of the mandir. These days he sat under the satiana tree beyond the temple complex. Hearing him scream, many visitors believed that he was insane.

But Hanu was not mad. When hunger pangs became unbearable, Hanu's rage burst forth in torrents of abuse. The purohit could do nothing about it, except cover his ears and try to shut out the words. People visiting the temple for the first time threw stones at Hanu, as if he were a stray dog. This upset him further and he would make obscene gestures. Then there was no choice but to ignore him.

While Hanu was still working at the temple, the purohit had been kind to him – in his own interest, of course. Hanu had helped with his household chores. Besides, the hunchback also knew of the purohit's weakness for good food. A little secret about an alliance with a washerwoman added to Hanu's arsenal which he used mercilessly now, whenever he subjected the purohit to a volley of invectives. This was his way of assuaging his hunger and the pain of the festering wounds afflicting his body.

That morning too, Hanu started his tirade as soon as the purohit entered the temple. "Ai, you bastard, you dhobin's pimp! How dare you let someone else take my place? What have I done to harm you, you parasite? Have I poisoned your pond?"

The purohit tried to ignore the abuses. But after a while, he could not stand them any longer and came out to the verandah. Thank god there were no bhaktas around yet. He shouted back, "Ai, Hanu! Have you gone mad? Why are you soiling your mouth so early in the morning?"

Hearing this, Hanu let loose even more obscene abuses. The disgusted purohit covered his ears, saying, "Oh, you mahapaapi, you are soiling the Devi's mandir. In your next life, you'll surely be born a chandaal!"

Hanu laughed out loud. The purohit's outburst seemed to have amused him. "Ha, Ha! Why? Am I better off than a chandaal now? Do you want to know what I can foresee? Kites will peck at your shrivelled body! Now tell me, whom have you allowed to occupy my place? Answer. Answer, you who are about to die."

"Who am I to allow anyone to sit there? What is the Mandir Committee for? Go ask them. In fact," the purohit continued, "a shop is going to be set up in that corner. There will be a mela on the whole field. The Devi's glory will spread far and wide. Bhajans are to be sung in her praise for seven days and nights. The glorious Devi is pleased and there is to be a grand union of Shiva and Parvati. Whoever is lucky enough to witness this momentous occasion will bodily ascend to heaven. Not that an infidel like you would be so fortunate!"

Hanu spat at the purohit. The priest left the verandah in a huff, seeking refuge in the innermost sanctum of the mandir.

Ai, Hanu!" The voice held both admonition and sympathy. It worked like magic, for Hanu calmed down immediately. Wiping the spittle off his chin, he turned around and saw Ahalya standing there. A heavily made-up face. Hair parted in the middle, a broad band of sindoor in it. Ahalya was a prostitute. If Hanu listened to anybody, it was to Ahalya. Her house was in a corner of the market and she lived by selling her body. Hanu did not know how long she had been standing there, listening to his abuses. Now she reproached him, "Chee, Chee, Hanu. Did you have to pollute your mouth even before day-break?"

"Why are *you* out so early? Didn't you get any customers last night?" retorted Hanu.

Ahalya was nonchalant. "Who says business is bad? All these traders who have come for the mela ..."

"Mela? Why is the mela being held out of season, Ahalya?" Hanu recalled what the purohit had said and wanted to find out more. The mela usually took place in the dry season.

"You simpleton! Don't you know? The Devi has found a partner. And she will be going to her bridegroom's house soon," joked Ahalya.

Hanu could not believe this. "Be careful, Ahalya. Don't say such things."

But Ahalya was still in a playful mood, and continued, "Ha! When you talk rubbish before the Devi, then it's not a sin. But if I say something, it's wrong. Anyway, come. I've brought some malpua for you to eat."

Hanu retraced his steps to his place under the satiana tree. Ahalya followed, a little distance between them. Someone had stuck a few stakes in the ground there to mark the site for a shop. Hanu could feel a sudden surge of anger. Since Ahalya was there, he controlled his rage and moved to sit under another tree. The malpua doused the fire in his belly.

Ahalya and Hanu were old acquaintances. They had met many years ago. Though an ugly hunchback, Hanu had been young and virile then, with a newly-sprouted beard. While returning from the mela one day, he had found Ahalya half-dead – raped and abandoned by a gang of drunkards. He had taken her to his hut and nursed her back to life. But for him, she would have surely died. In return, she had gifted him some unforgettable moments one night – an introduction to the pleasures of adulthood. His experience of love-making was restricted to that one night. And he guarded it jealously, an experience to be savoured little by little in his thoughts alone.

Now that he was afflicted with the dreaded disease, Ahalya too avoided touching him. The sight of his abominably swollen body repulsed her. But she also felt sorry for him. She could understand a little of what the purohit could not. She realised that his behaviour was a reaction to his misfortune, born of his helplessness. It was an expression of his frustration. And the extent of his agony was such that even the Devi did not escape his ire. No one but Ahalya sympathised with him, which is why she often brought him food or some rags to cover his nakedness.

It was Hanu's belief that the mandir's Devi had been cruel and unjust to him. Otherwise why should he suffer like this – he, who had devoted his life to her and had played an important role in the building of the mandir? But for him, this stone-hearted Devi would not have been as important as she was.

It had happened when the pond was being dug – the one which had provided Hanu with a means of earning his livelihood. It was meant to be a convenient source of drinking water for visitors to the bazaar and the weekly haat. The hunchbacked, adolescent Hanu had been allowed to join in this good work.

One day, just as he had started to dig, Hanu's spade hit something hard, making a metallic sound. Quickly, he dug around it and found a carved stone idol of a devi. A part of the nose had been chipped off. Still, it was a devi's moorti. Hanu took it to the chairman of the Market Committee.

The news spread like fire. People thronged to the spot to see this miraculous find. Soon it was decided that a mandir would be built there. The Market Committee took on the responsibility of supervising the work. The moorti was first housed in a straw hut, then in a tin shanty, and finally in this concrete, pillared structure.

Gradually the mandir had become an important place of pilgrimage for the Devi's bhaktas. A mela began to be held there every year. With the increase in devotional fervour and the number of visitors to the temple, some elements meant to satisfy baser needs also made their surreptitious entry – small sheds serving liquor or bhang, and of course, women like Ahalya, who sold their bodies.

Since the Devi's nose was broken she could not be kept in full view of the devotees. So a light muslin cloth screened her from them. Only the purohit was permitted to see her, as he was in charge of the rituals. He would bathe the moorti and adorn it with flowers and ornaments. Benevolence and blessings poured forth from the veiled Devi in the dark sanctum. Her mysterious presence aroused the curiosity of the devotees and strengthened their faith. Legends of her powers spread.

Hanu had been associated with the temple right from the beginning – when this bountiful Devi was not so well-known. Initially it had been his duty to strike the gong in the morning to announce the opening of the doors of the mandir. Then he took on the exclusive task of supplying drinking water to thirsty pilgrims, earning a little money in the process. But now, that same Hanu was in this sorry situation.

Ahalya's malpuas had cooled Hanu's temper as well as his hunger. He was eager to find out more about the off-season mela. So he asked her again.

"I would have told you, but I didn't get a chance because you were so angry."

Ahalya told him that a Shiva linga had been found recently on a snake-infested hillock a little distance away. The linga, it seems, was a natural one – not fashioned by any human hand.

"Who found it?" Hanu wanted to know.

"I don't know. They say that the chairman of the Mandir Committee dreamt that this Shiva linga is our Devi's bridegroom.

She wishes to join him, it seems. She will stay on the hill for six months of the year, and spend the remaining six here."

The mela was being held to celebrate this union of Shiva and Parvati. In the dream, the Devi had promised that those bhaktas who were present at her wedding would be delivered from all suffering. Even sinners would be pardoned.

"The Devi and her bridegroom will be on the same platform for a fortnight and then be put on individual pedestals. The goddess has promised to bless anyone who witnesses the union. Hanu, if you can somehow be there, you might be cured!"

Breaking into loud guffaws, Hanu said, "Did you know I broke the nose of that heartless one? Unknowingly, of course! That's why she's punishing me now. Why should I go to enjoy her amorous adventure? But, what about you? I don't think you will be able to make it. Your business has picked up, you said."

Ahalya was shocked. "Are you mad? The Devi's listening. You shouldn't say such things, Hanu." She moved away quickly, before he could utter any more profanities.

Preparations for the mela picked up. It promised to be a big one. The whole area was alive with people and noise. Everything had to be just right for the puja. Expensive muslin of different qualities was brought from the big market far away. Hundreds of packets of agarbatti and dhoop were bought, mounds of the best quality Joha rice, ghee and spices were piled up – offerings for the Devi.

Groups of people from different areas set up camp. Their kirtan went on day and night, echoing in the surroundings. Other goods, too, were brought in for the mela. On bullock-carts, hand-pulled carts, even on motor-cycles. There were glass bangles, cosmetics, spurious medicines, brass and stone utensils, earthenware, aluminium pans and ladles, religious texts next to tales from the Arabian Nights and illustrated sex manuals. And almost on cue, came the palmists, showmen with monkeys and bears, magicians and bodybuilders – even a circus company.

Temporary sheds sprang up overnight, displaying their wares – vegetables, tamarind pulp, blue, red, and yellow sherbet. Also, delicacies like nimkin, gajja, and khurma, liberally garnished with flies. Mango and jackfruit pheriwalas came. And barbers. Attracted by all this, even more people visited the mandir. They thronged the temple grounds till about midnight. In the din, Hanu's loud voice almost went unheard. Ahalya did not have time to enquire after him. There was, however, no shortage of food for Hanu. Visitors often threw away food, half-eaten. So there was enough for him and the other beggars, though they had to fight for it.

But that did not stop Hanu from ranting. He could not join in the fun because of his physical condition. It made him even more irritable. Most of his abuse was directed at the purohit. But he did not spare the Devi and would describe her body in gutter language. The purohit's warnings, "You'll surely go to hell!" only served to increase the volume of the expletives. His disease saved him from a thrashing, perhaps even from being murdered by irate bhaktas.

A day before the Devi was due to leave for her bridegroom's house, the doors of the mandir were closed to the public. There were so many rituals to go through. The Devi had to be ceremonially bathed to make her more radiant for the occasion. She had to be decked in rich clothes and adorned with jewels. Then she would be placed in a beautiful palki, which was to be carried on a big-wheeled vehicle made to look like a rath. Accompanied by chants and kirtan, thousands of devotees would pull the rath to the hilly abode, where her husband – a block of stone – awaited her.

Once the doors of the temple were closed, the pilgrims thronged the mela. The courtyard of the mandir fell silent. The purohit and his assistants were busy with preparations for the next day's festivities. But the purohit was worried. He was afraid Hanu would defile the holy atmosphere. Fortunately, Hanu had stayed away till then.

Another problem occurred to the purohit. Suppose Hanu wanted to pull the rath with everyone else? The Devi had appeared in a dream and commanded that nobody was to be stopped from drawing the rath on that auspicious day. To overcome this problem, a separate rope was attached to the vehicle, though the purohit hoped Hanu would remain sullen and refuse to join them. At midnight, all the preparations were over. Everyone went home to rest. The mela, too, had broken up.

By dawn, the temple compound was teeming with people. The Devi was already in the palki, behind a beautiful muslin screen. It would not be removed till she was united with her bridegroom. She would be taken to the foot of the hill on the rath. From there, the members of the Committee would carry the palki on their shoulders. The purohit would accompany them, chanting mantras all the way. Bhaktas could follow the palki, at some distance.

The procession began to move forward slowly, led by the members of the Committee. The elated cries of the bhaktas rent the air. The sound of conch-shells and gongs added to the fervour. Women ululated. Kirtan singers beat their drums and clanged the cymbals. Holding on to the palki, the purohit sat on the rath.

They stopped about three kilometres away, at the foot of the hill. The palki was taken down, the Devi still behind the muslin screen. Even the purohit was not allowed to see her till she faced her bridegroom.

Carefully lifting the palki on to their shoulders, the leaders of the procession moved up the hill. The purohit and the devotees followed. It was an arduous journey. Steep. The path lined with thorny bushes. The fear of snakes. But the expectation of instant salvation egged them on. They huffed their way up, undeterred.

The stone, eight to nine feet high, was visible from quite a distance, standing majestically alone. It looked exactly like a Shiva linga. Eager to attain salvation, the bhaktas regarded this piece of stone as an unmistakable sign of Mahadeva. Their cries of praise reverberated in the sky and the space beyond.

Suddenly, the procession stopped. The chants were replaced by a deathly silence. The purohit was the first to discern the reason for this unnatural silence. A man sat cross-legged at the base of the Shiva linga, staring at them with bulging eyes.

"Hanu! You sinner! What are you doing here?" screamed the purohit, panic-stricken. "Get away. Move."

But Hanu sat there, unmoving. Absolutely still. The purohit inched forward cautiously. It was as he had suspected. Hanu was dead – had been dead for some time. He held something in his arms. What could it be? Oh my god! The Devi! Hanu must have stolen the broken-nosed moorti last night.

What then had they been carrying in the palki all this while? The palki was still on the shoulders of the carriers. Trembling with fear, the purohit rushed to it and pulled away the muslin screen. The crowd could see that it had accompanied a slab of stone. Hanu had placed the stone there in the dark of the night.

Terror chilled the blood of all present. To the Committee members, the palki suddenly seemed to weigh several maunds more. They dropped it abruptly. All eyes now turned to the huge stone, the embodiment of Shiva. In the play of sunlight, all they saw was a lifeless monolith, jutting into the sky, indifferent to their plight.

A stampede broke out. The terrified bhaktas rushed down the hill. A snake slithered down the side of the broken-nosed moorti in Hanu's arms, and disappeared.

translated by
Shampa Ghosh

All day long, Silak's father would sit on the wooden bench in the verandah. Ilbon, the wood-seller, lit a fire for him in the circular angta every evening. But the cold did not seem to get out of his bones.

Silak's father would lament to anyone who came by, "I sent my granddaughter to Calcutta to study and she has changed. But those days I had won so much money at the races, it went to my head. I didn't pay attention to what anyone said. Now the child has become a big problem." The neighbours sympathised with Silak's father, yet they could not help but be pleased. Silak's mother had been so arrogant, this was a just reward for her, they thought. Their only regret was that she hadn't lived long enough to see it. Silak's father was aware of all this. If only this girl would find a suitable husband and have children. But no! She won't let anyone even come near her. Sighing deeply, Silak's father

SILAK'S DAUGHTER

by Lila Majumdar

stood up. All the chill of the land seemed to gather in this part of Moulai.

Silak's father always had a bag hanging from his shoulder with his paan in it, so he did not have to disturb anyone when he wanted it. But even after putting the paan with a pinch of chuna and a whole supari into his mouth, he did not find any comfort. Suddenly his heart longed for Silak's mother. For twenty-five years she had kept him under strict control. Only once a year, at the time of the Nongkrem dance, would she allow him to go away. Otherwise she never let him out of her sight. What strength she had! She could beat him to a pulp. The old man's heart swelled with pride. She had been good-looking, too. Almost as tall as her husband, with thick, soft, dark-brown hair, which when left loose, cascaded down to her knees. But apart from her family, how many people had been fortunate enough to see it?

She had a great sense of propriety, Silak's mother. She would not allow her family to deviate from the customs and traditions of the land. She never wore white. Only the Udhkar women wore white. Not once had she thought of giving up her traditional dress. With a sigh, Silak's father thought of his dead wife in the high-necked jacket, with sleeves reaching the elbows, two pieces of mooga cloth tied behind her in an artistic knot, a dark-coloured scarf round her head. How beautiful she had looked in that old-fashioned costume! She had loved dressing up, too. Pure gold earrings which covered the whole ear, a necklace of gold and coral beads, each bead as large as a duck's egg. It was real coral, lifted from the heart of the ocean. In this land of mountains, no one had even seen the ocean those days. Except the few who went to France during the War. But how many of them came back?

Silak had not returned. She was that Silak's mother, and he, her husband. In the twenty-five years that they had been together, she had never once let him be unworthy of her. Had she been alive today, she would not have allowed him to sit here, huddled up like this. Immediately, Silak's father lowered his feet into his mustard-coloured boots and sat up straight.

The wind whistled through the long leaves of the saral tree, and a faint smell of incense wafted through the air. Folding up its wings, the day seemed to be getting ready to return to its nest. He suddenly started feeling hungry.

Whenever he felt hungry these days, Silak's father thought of his own mother. His father would spend his time drinking and sleeping, while his mother toiled, breaking stones, and earning six annas at the end of the day. A road was being constructed below Moulai, at Dhankheti. The area was a real dhan khet, a paddy field then, not crowded with houses. In one corner, was Kutuk Budho's hut. Baba! How frightened he had been of the old man. Night and day Kutuk Budho worked in the little garden around the house, growing potatoes and pumpkins. Behind the hut, a mountain stream gurgled its way over the stones.

In the afternoon the women labourers would take an hour's break to eat their lunch of rice. How sweet was the taste of that rice! His younger brother Khullung, tied to his mother's back, would not want to climb down from there the whole day. Only when he fell asleep would his mother put him on the ground under a tree. Beside him, she would keep a big bowl of rice, covered with a dirty piece of cloth. And there would be plantains for Khullung, with the seeds still in them. Whenever he cried he would have to be fed the mashed plantains. What a fat child Khullung had been! Silak's father could hardly lift him.

After that it would be time for his lunch. A big bowl of thick-grained rice and a little red hot charchari of dried fish – the taste of it was heavenly. His mother would take him down to the river and wash his face and hands. She would cup her hands and fill them with water for him to drink. From her shoulder-bag she would take out paan, supari and a tin of chuna, tear off the stalk of the paan leaf and hand it to him.

Suddenly the sharp, pungent taste of the paan stalk came back to his tongue. At that moment Silak's father yearned for his childhood.

There was Kusmi! Proper paved steps lead up from the foothills, going past someone's kitchen or skirting another's storage shed. As you came up you could ask after everyone's well-being. But the girl never took the steps. Not for her the path on which her mother and grandmother had walked.

Kusmi came up and called out, "Dada!" Both cheeks were tinged with red. She was panting slightly and even on that winter evening there were beads of sweat on her forehead. Kusmi was wearing a green sari. On her wrists glittered two thick, bangles of pure gold.

"What are you staring at, Dada?" she asked.

"I suddenly remembered that there, where the pine trees hide the moonlight from one's eyes, the tiger traps are laid. Why do you come home so late, Kusmi? Aren't you afraid of anything?"

A slight smile lit up the corners of Kusmi's eyes. She pulled out two large silver pins from her hair. Thick, straight, soft as silk, her brown hair cascaded to her knees. An ache rose in the old man's throat. "Why did you return so late, Kusmi?" he grumbled. "Where did you go? Don't you know that I feel hungry at this time?"

Kusmi came up to him and hugged him. "Were you worried, Dada? Why do you become like this as soon as it is dark? There are no tigers now."

How suddenly the dusk falls in this land. As soon as the sun sets behind those bare mountains in the distance, clouds of darkness descend to earth and lie in thick layers all around. Fireflies glint among the trees, the chirping of crickets breaks the stillness of the night and the street dogs echo the howl of the jackals. The huge bats attack each other as they flock to the wild-pear tree to eat the fruit. Then they spread their wings like dark umbrellas and melt into the blackness of the forest. In the night, the distant forest seems to crowd in, and the deep purple, star-studded sky to press down.

Silak's father felt suffocated. No words escaped his lips. He just managed to say, "It's not good to stay up so late, Kusmi. In the old days, we had dinner and went to bed as soon as dusk fell. There was great danger outside."

Kusmi put her loving arms around the old man's neck. Her hair curtained his face. In the light of the kerosene lamp Silak's father could see red glints in the brown tresses. A beautiful fragrance arose from them. His turban slipped off and his head felt cold. Kusmi laughed and caressed his bald head. "If you are afraid of the dark, Dada," she whispered in his ear, "why did you build your house at the edge of the forest?"

But no, it wasn't Silak's father who had built the house. Things were different those days. A man lost his prestige if he did an ordinary job. If he joined the army, or at least the police force, that was all right. Silak's father had never done any work, but even so, he was widely respected. In the five hill regions around, there were few men who could equal him in archery. At the Nongkrem dance festival, when he rode on his horse, a colourful, fringed turban on his head, the girls stared at him with enchantment in their eyes. And the men watched him with envy in their hearts.

This house had been built by Silak's mother's mother. They were all dead and gone now. Only Silak's father has been left behind. Strong as ever, he hasn't lost a single tooth yet!

L et's go inside, Kusmi. I'm hungry."

Ilbon had cooked chicken curry, and put a couple of eggs into the rice. Silak's father didn't notice any of this.

"Why won't you marry Domor, Kusmi?" he asked. "Do you know that he is a descendant of the kings of this land? Till recently we were their subjects. We gave them a portion of the harvest, also a share of the fowls. It's your good fortune that he wants to marry you. Tell me why you won't marry him."

Kusmi turned her eyes away from Silak's father's face. "What's the hurry, Dada?"

"Why the delay, Kusmi? You have finished your studies and come home. Everybody said you wouldn't come back. Once she gets a taste of Calcutta, they said, she won't be able to settle down here. Why won't you get married? If only you marry Domor and stay near me!

I don't have any strength in my legs these days, Kusmi."

The light from the kerosene lamp fell on Kusmi's face. Brown eyes sparkled brightly below thin arched eyebrows. High cheekbones, a small straight nose, bright red lips like the petals of a rose, and long reddish brown hair spread over her back.

"If you don't feel strong, Dada, why don't you have a little milk?" Kusmi asked.

When he was young, no one ever drank milk. As soon as babies were weaned, they would start eating plantains. How sweet was the taste of those plantains! Ma would take the seeds out of them and Silak's father and Khullung would lick the plantains from her hand. Nothing tasted as sweet nowadays. Silak's father pushed his plate away and got up.

Through the glass panes of the shuttered windows, he stared at the world outside. A cool breeze was blowing. The long grass on either side of the road swayed, the stars twinkled. How beautiful it was. How white. How cool. How lonely!

Silak's father shivered involuntarily.

"Don't go off to sleep now, Dada," Kusmi said. "It's not good to fall asleep immediately after a meal. Here, come and sit beside the angta and stretch your legs." Then after a slight pause, she continued, "Dada, what kind of a man was my father, Silak?"

Silak's father could remember nothing about Silak. Sometimes he asked the neighbours. They were surprised, but even they did not remember him very well.

"He died in the War, in France," said Silak's father.

"That much I know," Kusmi replied impatiently. "'I know he was very wild. He caused great unhappiness to both of you. Without telling anyone he married a girl from a different caste. Then I was born. Didima was furious. She had a fight with him. In his anger, Baba went and enlisted in the army. He went off to France." With a deep sigh Kusmi continued, "But what sort of a man was he? What kind of a woman was my mother?"

Silak's father was upset. "Who knows what sort of man he was! This much I can say – he was very naughty. He broke that big bow of mine for no reason ... How can I say what sort of man he was? Must have been a handsome fellow ... He looked down upon the local girls. He used to say that the mountain girls with their short bodies, flat noses and thick ankles were no good. He went and married a girl from another caste, from Nongpo ... Yes! Now I remember. They returned home one evening like this. He was standing at the doorstep, the girl waited outside. Every now and then, he pulled his collar closer around him. It was very cold. I felt sorry for them. But his mother would not let them enter the house. She drove them away."

Silak's father looked around distractedly. Then his eyes fell on Kusmi and he said, "Are you crying, Kusmi? I told you he was very naughty and disobedient. He was only twenty years old but he was as proud as he was stubborn. Afterwards, to console me, his mother would say, Such a son deserves to be turned away ... Do you know, I never saw him again. I can't even remember his face."

"Why didn't you tell me all this till now, Dadu?" asked Kusmi with a catch in her throat.

"Who knows! Maybe I had forgotten it."

"What happened after that?"

"They lived in a room beside a shop in Lumparing for two months. Then he went off to France and never returned."

"After that?"

"It was all so long ago, I don't remember ... You were born. Your grandmother heard of the birth of a girl, and she went to see you. In those days no one ventured out after dark. But as soon as Silak's mother heard the news, she set off."

Outside, the cold wind whistled and the jackals howled.

"And you?" Kusmi asked in a choked voice.

"I also went with her."

"What happened then?"

"From the bed where she lay, your mother had a raging fight with her. By that evening your mother was also dead. Your grandmother plucked you from your dead mother's bosom and brought you here. We walked all the way in the darkness, neither of us saying a word. After that ... I don't remember anything more ... Kusmi, when you cry, it breaks my heart." Silak's father's hands trembled as he tried to pull Kusmi to him.

"No, Dadu, I won't cry. But what about you? You didn't feel sad then? You didn't cry? Don't you feel sorry that you never saw your twenty-year old son again?"

Silak's father shook his head very slowly. "I don't know." Huge teardrops rolled down his cheeks. "I don't remember anything of those days, Kusmi."

The wind shrieked outside.

"Dada," Kusmi said, "I too love a boy from another community." She raised her eyes to look at the old man's face. "If you allow him, he will come and meet you."

"But ... but ..." Silak's father mumbled. "Where does he stay? What is his name? What does he do?"

"He teaches at the missionary school in Laimokhra. His name is Alok. We were in college together in Calcutta. He is a Bengali ... But it's all right, Dada. If you are unhappy about it, I'll tell him to go away. Don't worry."

"You will tell him to go away?"

"I thought I would have to quarrel with you today! Why are there tears in your eyes, Dadu?"

Silak's father pulled out a dirty handkerchief from his pocket, wiped his eyes and blew his nose. Silak's mother had been so particular about cleanliness!

Kusmi stood up.

"You don't have to worry about anything, Dada. I'll tell him to go away."

Silak's father carefully folded the handkerchief and put it in his pocket. With the back of his right hand he rubbed his eyes. Then he said, "No. Tell him to come and meet me."

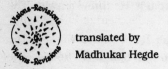

translated by
Madhukar Hegde

THE CHEST

by Shirish Panchal

Madhav had never liked the evening rain. Rain in the evening was unfair! He did not mind if it poured during the night and he woke up to a sky wringing itself out. In a way it was better that the rain had spent its force. A light shower was good for the crops. Madhav remembered the time when he had worked in the field in the drizzle. His feet would sink into the mud, soft after the night rain. When he returned home, he would wash his feet with water from the copper pot outside, gently scrubbing them to get the mud off. How he enjoyed that! Those little pleasures had gone forever. Finished.

Rain! Madhav had loved it. As he entered the house, the water would be cascading from the reverberating tin roof. Buckets and pans placed below the sloping kitchen roof would fill up and overflow. Now, all that seemed to be a part of a previous birth.

He lit a bidi and took a long,

deep puff. But he got no satisfaction from it. He threw it away. The tobacco had become too damp.

He glanced into the house. Deewali had gone to work at the housing society nearby with their younger daughter, Roopa. The two older children, Mahesh and Sharada, were at school. Madhav was alone in the empty, quiet house. Actually, even when everyone was there, he had enough space to himself. The other people had very small houses. Like him, they too had left their villages and come to this town ten, fifteen years ago. But how many had been able to afford a two-and-a-half room accommodation like his? Maybe it wasn't a good area – but Madhav had never lived in a "good" area. They considered him extremely fortunate, but he had not liked it when they moved here and he did not like it now. What was there in it to like?

Madhav's eyes once again panned his house. A few plants in broken pots. Wheat sprouting in small tins. Deewali had cultivated this hobby after she started working at the society. Madhav could see the wheat shoots in front of him. But he did not feel like touching them. In the fields, as soon as the shoots appeared, he would gently run his fingers over them, feel the tender leaves, play with them for hours. But here everything was dull, uninteresting. There was no magic left, no charm. Even the saali bidi tasted of kerosene. You could light one, two, three ... It made no difference.

The surroundings got on Madhav's nerves. He was upset by the plants being grown in a handful of mud. Mahesh had not liked them either and so he got up early one morning and flung them out. Deewali had thrashed him soundly. "Mara roya! Did you have to throw them away? Isn't it enough that we have been thrown out of our home?"

How much had changed in ten years, Madhav thought. Then, you could see nothing but fields. The tall neem, the spreading mango trees with their boughs almost kissing the earth, bawal trees along the edge of the fields, wells with leather water pouches, and sheltering everything, the open sky. He had lost touch with all that.

What else could he have done? Their resources had diminished over the years and the effort to make both ends meet had broken his back. Take up other jobs, people had said to him. But where were the jobs? He had no choice but to sit idle like everyone else – smoking bidis, staring at each other's vacant eyes. Occasionally, one of them would ask a question, then silence would reign again. Doing nothing for six months in the year had been frustrating. Finally, he had made up his mind without taking anyone's advice. Leaving his fields in another's care, he sold all that he could and came to the town. It was hard for them to leave behind the vast expanse of earth and sky. Their hearts were scarred and cracked, like the earth was, in times of drought. Deewali had sobbed her eyes out.

Madhav tried, but he just could not forget the past. Every now and then, those memories returned to haunt him, and the pain came back. Nothing pleased him. Except Deewali. He would lose himself and his memories in the labyrinth of her body. But even then he would mutter, "You have become like a burnt-out bidi. There's no pleasure to be had from you anymore." Deewali would push him away in mock anger and say, "A man who has only one eye may not be satisfied with what he sees, but he has to manage with it!" And Madhav would tell himself, as he peered into the cracked mirror, If she is like a spent bidi, you are no better. How he had let himself go! His beard was like the rough stalks in the fields after the harvest. His hair was stiff and prickly like porcupine needles and his lips had darkened from too much smoking.

Again Madhav looked up at the rain. He did not feel like going to his tea stall in the market-place. There would hardly be any customers anyway. To walk through this river of mud – the episode in the Puranas, of crossing a river of mud must have been something like this, he thought, his lips drawn into a sneer and his eyes hard.

There was mud in the village too, everywhere – on the path to the fields, the streets, the courtyard. But walking through that clean mud had never put him in a foul mood or brought an abuse to his lips. He did not mind holding it in his hands, or rubbing his body with it when he bathed, the early morning sun shining on him. But this mud? Chee! People, cows, buffaloes urinated and defecated all over the place, women washed vessels and threw garbage anywhere they pleased. To have to trudge through that ...

He would have sat there, grumbling, if Deewali had not come back then. The little one had stayed behind at the society. Deewali was drenched in the rain. She quickly went in, changed, and came and stood in front of Madhav. When he said nothing, she shrugged her shoulders and flounced off, to stand in front of the mirror. Making a chandlo on her forehead, she said, "My god, this rainy season doesn't end. I am fed up."

"Hn," Madhav started to reply but stopped, remembering what he had been thinking about earlier. He had not enjoyed the bidi either. Deewali looked at Madhav but there was no expression on his face. "God only knows what those hags saw in him when they named him Madhav. There is nothing pleasant about this face," she muttered.

"Get me some hot ukadu. I'll drink it and then go."

Deewali was moving towards Madhav. She was miserable and cold and this Madhav had asked for hot ukadu! She went back and took a matchbox from the shelf to light the stove. The matchbox was damp. She could not find another one. "Give me a matchbox. This one is damp. Everything is damp here," she shouted, as she began to pump the stove.

Through the open door, Madhav looked at her with a resigned expression. In the beginning, he used to get very angry at the slightest provocation and sputter like mustard seeds put into smoking oil. He even beat her up sometimes. But gradually he had got used to her sharp tongue. He could bear her barbs now. Nothing ever provoked him.

Madhav pushed aside the sack that covered the old chest in

the corner. He was about to open it, when he stopped. Instead of taking a matchbox from inside it, he stood there staring at it, his beloved majoos. His fatigue and irritation disappeared. His eyes lit up. A kind of energy rushed through his blood as he began to run his hands over the majoos. It was a long time since he had caressed even Deewali with such affection.

On their wedding night, after untying the strings of Deewali's pearl-studded kamkhani, he had touched her all over. In the smoky light of the lantern, and the all-pervading smell of kerosene, he had glimpsed her grayish dark back and had felt a fluttering sensation all over his body. He felt the same thrill once again. He forgot the rain, the town, the tea stall, Deewali ... It had been quite a job bringing this four-and-a-half foot wide, three-foot high, intricately carved, real sisam majoos, from the village to the town.

"Look at my rival later. First take out the matchbox!" Deewali shouted from the kitchen.

Madhav lost his temper. He glared at her, nostrils flaring, lips quivering. She was sitting in front of the stove, her sari pulled up to her knees. Hardly noticing her bare legs, he opened the majoos and threw a matchbox at her. Deewali struck a match and put it to the stove. There was too much kerosene and immediately, it blazed. "Mind your hair. It'll catch fire!" he said angrily.

Deewali quickly moved back.

Madhav's eyes returned to the open majoos. His uncle had said to him, "You don't know where you are going to stay. Where will you keep this big majoos?" But Madhav had already fixed up a place and had gone back to the village for Deewali. Everyone tried hard to dissuade him from lugging the majoos along. For a brief moment he did consider leaving it behind, but then he said, "No, Kaka. I must take it with me."

Deewali too had created a fuss. "Yes, yes. Take it with you. Hang it round your neck. Why don't you live in it?"

"Be quiet, woman. I'm taking you, aren't I?"

"You have to. You married me. But you want to take that whore of yours also."

Madhav had been so angry, he would have hit her with whatever he could lay his hands on, but for his uncle's presence.

M adhav had seen the majoos from his childhood. At first, in the dim glow of oil lamps, then in the light of lanterns and now in the glare of electric bulbs. He remembered all the stories his mother had told him about it. "Your mama used to say that the carving on our majoos is like the carving at Mount Abu. It was brought by your dadi from her father's house and it has been in our family for four generations. Look after it."

Madhav had always remembered those words. He and Deewali had moved from village to village, from town to town. Even in this town, they had changed several houses. Finally they had come to this two-and-a half room home. And the majoos had found a place for itself.

One by one, Madhav took out the contents of the majoos and spread them around. Matchboxes, small and big tea packets, pieces of old benarasi saris and heavily embroidered cloth. Suddenly, his thoughts galloped ... If Deewali was sitting in front of him wearing these beautiful things ...

Deewali brought him the ukadu. "What's this nonsense? How many times will you take things out and put them back? There is nothing in there!" she said sharply.

"How can I make you understand?" Madhav said, looking at her. "Come, share my ukadu."

"I have kept some for myself."

"Then bring it. We'll drink it together."

At once, Deewali's anger subsided. But she still pretended to be offended. She went in, poured the ukadu into a cup and came out. Madhav pulled her close. He looked first at Deewali, then at the majoos. "Often, I tell myself, Who do we have in this city? Let us sell everything and go back. We will manage somehow. How can I explain it to you? I miss the village. Sitting in the tea stall, watching the tea boil, I seem to have become like a broken cup-and-saucer myself."

Deewali looked long and deep into his eyes. Rarely did they get an opportunity to sit like this in the daytime. She thought, He may have become like a teacup, selling tea, but there is still a spark in him. Didn't his eyes brighten when I walked in just now?

She remembered their wedding. Sometime between Vasant Panchami and Holi she had applied haldi on her hands and put kesuda flowers in her hair. Hadn't his eyes lit up then too, when he saw her fragrant body?

She thought, What if he opened me up, the way he opened the majoos? Her eyes grew soft and seductive, like mahua flowers. But Madhav was in no mood to be intoxicated. Deewali stroked his head and said, "You are missing so much, aren't you?"

"What do you mean?"

"I can't satisfy you," she added, moving closer and peering into the majoos with him.

"Are you mad? You take care of most of my desires. Some needs are mental. Those that are unfulfilled, disappear when I look at this majoos. When you sow seeds, is it only the seed that sprouts? Whatever is buried in the field and whatever is stored in the earth also blooms. You think that this is only a patara. To me it is much more than that. Sometimes I think of it as a massive house with seven or eight rooms, opening up one by one. Or it is a seven-storeyed palace with each storey representing one generation."

"Will you ever be able to live without it?"

"We have given up so many things – the open sky, our precious lands, the tamarind trees at the edge of the fields, our homes – but as long as I have this majoos, I feel I have everything."

Deewali understood only some of what Madhav had said. He was highly educated by village standards, and had even gone to college for one year, while she had barely read seven books. Also Madhav had travelled a lot with his grandfather. At the age of nine or ten he had been to Hardwar, Kashi, Rameshwar and Ujjain.

"You can keep sitting here with your thoughts. I am going in to cook," said Deewali. She felt that Madhav would pull her sari and ask her to stay. But he just sat there quietly, staring at the majoos.

He felt better in this house. The first one had given him a lot of heartburn. It was as if the terrace, the courtyard, the compound, the whole village house, had been cramped into a room as small as a water tank. Whichever way you turned, you banged into a wall. They had moved from one rented room to another. Time passed, amidst Deewali's grumbling, the dust of Vaishakh, the leaking roof of Ashadh, the little oil-lamps in the mud pots at Navratri.

Winter came, and even Deewali's thinned-down body seemed as warm as the ashes of a burnt out fire. Like the village dogs who huddled in the ashes, he would cuddle up to Deewali. Her body was for him the warm days of Holi, the only silver lining to the clouds. It was the only thing that had kept him going.

Three times they had moved, before they found this two-and-half room house. He had to sell one field to buy it, illegally. He wasn't the only one who had done so. There were sixty to seventy such houses on that piece of land. The light and water connections had swallowed Deewali's two-tola gold chain. Regular manual labour, part-time jobs and hawking goods had led him to his present tea stall business. It seemed to get him more money than farming. But his stall was in an area that hardly attracted any customers after six o' clock in the evening. He would close the stall as soon as it started to get dark, and go home, to put all the day's earnings – clinking coins, dirty notes – into Deewali's hands. In the beginning he had enjoyed counting the money but soon he lost interest in it. He would open the majoos and sit in front of it. Just looking at it gave him great satisfaction. It made him forget all the difficulties he had to go through.

The majoos was balanced on bricks placed at each corner. Along three sides of its base, were delicately carved creepers and leaves. In the middle there was a row of peacocks and parrots in fine filigree work, and a little above that, small squares of brass were embedded in the carving. There were seven compartments of various sizes inside it. Whenever he opened the majoos, Madhav would see all that was inside it, and even what was not. And his eyes would light up.

It did not stop raining that day, so Madhav did not go to his tea stall. His routine changed completely after that. He spent less and less time at the tea stall and he started coming home early, to sit alone, and stare at the majoos.

Gradually, he began to hear sounds – from the cracks in the walls, from the doors, from the roof. All kinds of sounds – heavy, soft, shrill, sweet ... Toys, soap, shoes and slippers, biscuits, sherbet, clothes, toothpaste, chocolate, television. All the goods in the world were advertised loudly, assaulting his ears. He would have liked the silence of the grave better.

Madhav finally understood the real reason for the clamour for electricity, for which all of them had spent three, four thousand rupees. Everyone wanted a TV at home. His son was seven years old and the daughters were five and three. Their eyes, noses, tongues, ears were alert to these sounds. If they were asleep, they would wake up. If they were studying they would put aside their books, if they were talking they would stop. halfway and run to the neighbour's house, and it was difficult to make them come home. They didn't want datun so toothpaste arrived. Earlier milk with a little tea in it was fine, but now they wanted cocoa or chocolate. Following this was the demand for ice cream. Deewali also was influenced by the children. Madhav was forced to keep his tea stall open longer to take care of the extra expenses. Dust started gathering on the majoos.

But Madhav felt that something was wrong. His children didn't talk to him. Even Deewali was sulking most of the time. Very often no one was at home when he returned. Deewali would have gone to the neighbour's house and would come back only after half-past nine. He was forced to sit alone. He smoked bidis, one after the other. Sometimes he would wander around outside, his head heavy from breathing the fumes of the boiled tea. He wanted Deewali. That Deewali, dry and withered, with the crumpled pallav, uncombed hair, a strong smell of hing about her, holding the pot of water – he needed her near him. But she wasn't there. The loneliness hit him, almost broke him. The house reminded him of the fields in the evening – empty, deserted. He would stare at the majoos for hours till his eyes blurred and he saw not one majoos but two.

One night, when Deewali was lying in his arms, she brought up the subject. "I don't like to go to someone else's house everyday. You are left alone here."

Madhav squeezed her and murmured, "After a long time you are thinking of me."

"What to do? These children don't listen. The eldest keeps chanting TV-TV the whole day. Why don't we get a TV too?"

Madhav's hand stopped caressing Deewali's face. "What? Get a TV? From where? Shall I sell my stall? Sell another field, or sell you?" He was furious. But slowly he realized that what Deewali had said was true. The family could watch TV together. The children could do their lessons watching it. They could eat their food in front of it. He had heard that they show everything quite openly sometimes. It would be nice to see it, holding Deewali ... Let's buy a TV. Never mind if it's small. And so what if its not colour, Madhav thought.

Seeing Madhav's face, Deewali's eyes began to dance. Multi-coloured dreams flashed before her eyes.

"What happened?" she asked him, as she bit his ear. Madhav let out a squeal.

"I also think that we should buy a TV. But how? Even for an old one we will need a couple of thousands."

"Only two thousand?" Deewali was surprised.

"We will buy a black-and-white. A colour one will be more expensive."

Deewali slipped away. "Who buys black-and-white these days? Everyone has a colour set."

Madhav pulled the sulking Deewali into his arms again. "When we don't have much money, we have to manage somehow."

"Not possible." Deewali was adamant. After a short silence, she whispered softly, "If you listen to me we can get one without spending anything."

"What? Without money? Absolutely free?"

"Where I am working, the people want to give away their set. It is hardly two years old."

"Then? You will have to spend your whole life working for them to pay the money back."

"No, no. It's not like that. Listen to me at least. Once I had brought the lady from the house here."

"To our house?"

"I showed her our majoos. She was very happy when she saw it."

"So?" Madhav felt his stomach tighten.

"The majoos at their place, the TV at ours."

Madhav couldn't breathe. He felt as if somebody had set fire to the majoos. Or it had been stolen. Or that someone was bidding for it in the auction.

"You really are a thick-headed fool," Deewali said impatiently. "A TV like that would cost at least ten to twelve thousand. The lady is a collector of old things and that is why she has agreed. Which fool would give you ten thousand for your patara? I had to praise that rival of mine so much before she thought of buying it."

Madhav stood up. He went to the majoos. He peered at it and ran his fingers lovingly over the carving. How could Deewali even think of it? Madhav started abusing her.

"You bitch! Mention this again and I will cut you up and fill salt in your wounds. Did your father give it to you?"

Deewali cried and cried. For four days she went around with a glum face.

Every time he thought of what Deewali had suggested, Madhav's eyes blazed with fury. He felt as if a part of his body had been torn off. He sat in front of the majoos. Sometimes he saw fleeting images of his ancestors in it. Sometimes it turned into an advertisement for soap, tea, shoes, chappals, biscuits, a cycle, a motor-cycle ... and he felt he was on it, going round and round in the "Well of Death" in a circus, with Deewali sitting behind him, her heart thudding against his back.

In his childhood he had heard stories of the djinn who gave you whatever you asked for. Now, he only had to say Open and the majoos would open. All sorts of wonderful things would spill out of it – things to eat, to wear, to sleep on. Even things you didn't need. How much the majoos could hold! Every evening it would spill out its goodies. You only had to press a switch and they would all go away. Till the next day when again it would say, "Your wishes are my command."

Madhav's head started spinning. The two-and-a half room house had turned into a big shop. There was light everywhere from hundred, two hundred, five hundred watt bulbs, like the big shops in the cities. You could buy everything there ... For a moment he forgot what such shops were called. The people in these shops were from another world. They employed so many people to sell their goods. Pretty young girls with bright eyes.

Many days went by. Madhav could not sleep.

It was true. After all, what would he do with a patara? How long was he going to live in the past? What was wrong in exchanging it for a TV? The TV was like the magic tree, the one the gods had, which granted wishes.

One morning Madhav told Deewali. And she, before he could change his mind, took the majoos to the lady's house. And brought the TV home. Everyone was thrilled. Deewali distributed pedas. No cooking was done. Food was brought from outside. That night, Deewali's body revealed unimagined delights to Madhav.

Madhav kept muttering, "Ask, Ask. And it's yours."

translated by
Premila Condillac

Even as he sat there, Amit knew that Parul was combing her hair, more like tugging at it, in the inner room. That done, she would wind it ruthlessly around her hand and slap a tight bun on to her head. And then, jab eight or ten pins into it, here and there ... almost as if it was someone else's hair. Amit was aware that the irritation and anger constantly simmering within Parul were because of him and directed at him. But he sat secure in his rhino-like armour. Barbs directed at him bounced back and hurt her, while he basked in the warm glow of victory.

After she had put on her saree, Parul would carefully apply a "foundation" of good-naturedness on her face ... layer upon thick layer of measured sweetness and pasted smiles. No one who looked at her could ever imagine the many conflicts that were raging within her at various levels of her being. It was not that she was such a fine actress. Rather, it was the

NAYAK
KHALNAYAK ♦ VIDUSHAK

by Mannu Bhandari

result of a large dose of gentility and decorum that had been forced down her throat at birth, and which did not permit her to do anything as crude as show her grief.

Well, Parul could fool the world, but not Amit. Only he knew the abuses and curses that lay behind the loving words and honeyed tones with which she addressed him in the presence of others. Civility, gentility ... nothing but the cheap props of a life of duplicity and hypocrisy! His lips twisted in bitter mockery. Just as well he had dealt with their boring and oppressive "sophistication" right in the beginning – chomped, digested and deposited it where it belonged! His chest swelled with pride once more at the thought.

Picking up a sheet of chart paper, Amit sat down to finish the sketch of a stage-set with such total absorption that it was as if the world had ceased to exist for him outside of his work ... Parul, at any rate, had.

Even with his eyes glued to the paper, his back "saw" that Parul had drawn the curtain aside and was standing in the doorway, wondering how to leave politely without saying a word. Even if she was in no mood to talk, her sense of wifely duty would compel her to say something, at least an "OK, I'm going." The word "office" would, of course, never be uttered in the presence of her unemployed husband. That would be in such poor taste! Her genteel upbringing acknowledged the importance of handling a husband's self respect with care.

"Will you be home at around four today?"

The question took him by surprise. He looked up, despite himself. Wah! His guess had been perfect. She stood there all dressed up, looking so young and fresh. Who would imagine that this woman had spent the previous night turning and tossing in bed? He might have had his back towards her, but he knew that she had been shedding tears all night. Hats off to her!

Surely, there must be some special "training" which equipped people with the ability to hide their emotions. Or else why was it that, hardly had a thought entered his mind, and his face, in fact every damn hair on his body, seemed eager to announce it to the whole world? This in spite of his being an accomplished actor. But what could he do? After all, his parents had sent him to a municipal school to learn to read and write ... from where was he to acquire this "super-sophistication" of the "convent" types?

"Amma will be coming here ... if you are at home, she'd like to meet you."

He had half a mind to say, Thanks for the honour you have bestowed on me by using if. You could've simply ordered, Be at home at four and sit and talk to Amma. A good-for-nothing like you would have nowhere to go, anyway. But no. I apologise. Such crass words were not to be found in her vocabulary, however ugly the thoughts that were churning in her mind.

"Don't upset your plans on her account. Amma has to come this side for some work in any case."

"What does she want to speak to me about?"

"I don't know. I didn't ask and she didn't offer to tell me. All she said on the phone was, Will Amit be at home at four o'clock? Tell him I'll see him if he is." Then, ever so casually, she added, "What could it be? She probably wants to drop by for a chat since she is coming this way."

Oh that flippant air! She shouldn't try it on him. Why didn't she come right out and say that her mother was planning to set him right, to let him know that, having married her darling daughter, he would have to mend his irresponsible ways?

"Breakfast is ready. Ask for it while you are working or whenever you like – Regular eating habits are beyond you of course – All right then, I'm off." The faintest trace of a mild perfume wafted past him. Really, nothing would ever make these people give up their airs!

Exit heroine. Now he was free till the entry of Ammaji, the villain. Freedom! Liberation! He tossed his pencil in the air, stretched langorously and took a couple of deep breaths. "Murari," he called out loudly, "One coffee. Make it piping hot." With that he sprawled out on the bed, completely at ease.

What a relief! How trapped and suffocated he had been feeling all this while! In spite of his resistance, these two were taking charge of his life, destroying his identity. They seemed to have become his destiny. A sharp wave of pain washed over him as he recalled his old room – untidy, chaotic, yet a place where he had felt like a king even in times of abject penury. And the narrow gali, visible from the one solitary window, had been nothing less than a boulevard to his eyes.

Now that the daughter had exhausted her arsenal in a futile bid to domesticate him, Ammaji was going to try her hand at it. All right, let her come – he would deal with her too. They both needed to be put in their places, and his rightful position had to be hammered into their heads. The matter must be settled once and for all.

She must be planning to strike him down with deceptive, sugar-coated cunning. So that he, already weighed down by her favours, would be rendered helpless by her kindness. Ammaji must have assumed that a few sentences would be enough to set this spoilt brat right. She could then return home victorious, banners flying high.

Ammaji's daughter had begun to consider herself an artiste after just a few roles – which he had given her – and by playing around with the arrangement of cushions and curtains in the house. No longer, though. Now she clearly understood the pride and the ego of the true artist. That love of freedom which he would not barter for the greatest luxuries (trivial as they were, in his opinion, in any case). Ammaji would also get a glimpse of this truth now.

As for matters of dialogue and style, who could compare with him, a born actor? These required not good-breeding but talent – an attribute that he, not Ammaji, possessed in abundance. This encounter was sure to be a knock-out for him!

Just the thought filled Amitosh with a new self-confidence. He felt as if a strange power was being born within him, shaking him out of the lethargy that had overcome him of late and adding a new weight to his personality. The surge of self-confidence brought with it a clarity of mind which allowed him to anticipate the many allegations which his mother-in-law was sure to make, and to effortlessly formulate hard-hitting rejoinders. Not content with having his lines ready, he even went so far as to rehearse them a few times with full theatrical effects.

Now he was ready for battle. This mother-and-daughter team had overestimated its power. He would show them where they stood with him. The ongoing cold war against his lifestyle, his habits and, most importantly, his freedom (the freedom of an unbridled bull if their unspoken thoughts were to be put in words) must come to an end. Let the final curtain fall!

He waited impatiently for the curtain to rise, in eager anticipation of the moment when he would finally bring it down. Time suddenly began to hang heavy on his hands and he picked up a book. Normally by now, having eaten a good meal, he would be stretched out on the bed and would fall asleep with Parul's unexpressed dictum ringing in his ears, "Only the slothful have the good fortune to sleep during the day." He'd left the door open. In response to the faint knocking, "Come in," he said.

And the villain came onstage. The same dignified appearance, the same gentle smile – truly her daughter's mother in every respect. Almost as if they were not flesh and blood at all, but dolls created from the same mould. No wonder they could not understand what "personality" means, or the power of a strong individual.

"Oh good! I'm glad I found you at home. I thought you might have gone out to some rehearsal. I had spoken to Parul but there was no way of knowing ... So, I had to take a chance."

Amitosh was silent.

"It's been so long since you all came over. (A sugar-coated reproach). I know you're very busy but do spare some time for this lonely soul. You know how I fret when I don't see you two for a while."

Amit was silent, but words took shape in his mind ... If I may be so bold as to put in my own language, the essence of what you are really saying, which lies not in these honeyed words of yours but in what remains unsaid, it is this – An unemployed person cannot be short of time. It is just that you don't want to visit me. You avoid me. And thanks to you, poor Parul can't come over either. All day she slogs in her office ... if she were to come and sit with me in the evenings it would give you open licence to fool around.

As his mother-in-law passed her gaze over the room, her face came alive and her eyes lit up with appreciation. "So Parul has put up the new curtains – they certainly make the room more cheerful. She has always been so fond of doing up the house." And then continued in doting tones, "Some may accuse me of constantly praising my own daughter but this much I must say, very artistically inclined she is, this daughter of mine. Such an eye for choosing things. A real artist."

Good god! What an insult to art! For those unfamiliar with even the "a" of art, perhaps "real art" meant the ability to hang curtains, fold napkins and arrange cutlery on the table. Just as the bitter words were threatening to boil over, Ammaji produced her trump card.

"And the ultimate evidence of her good taste is the fact that she chose you, one of the top artists of the theatre world. In fact the best, I would say."

Though his hands did not move, Amit mentally clenched his fists. They were not going to work on him, these clever tactics she was using to try and douse his anger. He would not allow himself to cool down.

They both fell silent. It was as if each one was sizing the other up before getting to the heart of the matter.

"Amit, I have come to talk to you about something," she said in a voice stripped of all its earlier affection, its indulgence.

Hmm ... so now we're getting on to the right track. He was immediately on his guard. But then, another pause. Perhaps she was sharpening the cutting edge of the words she was going to use – precisely measured words they would be, and deadly sharp, so as to pierce him through and through.

"I don't quite know how to start."

Come on. At least have the good sense not to stage your theatrics before an actor. Why don't you just reel off the long list of my misdeeds which your daughter must have given you? You must have committed it to memory over these past few days. Where is the problem in starting? Oh, I see ... your delicate vocabulary has no words to describe my base deeds ... tch, tch ... truly a serious problem. Poor Amma!

"Parul had specifically told me not to talk to you about this, even inadvertantly, but ..."

Thank god, at least the daughter had realised that he was not one of those spineless creatures who are reduced to tail-wagging nobodys in the presence of these "superior" people.

"I couldn't let it rest ..."

Ah yes, a mother's love ... Couldn't bear to see her poor daughter suffer.

"After all, what can happen? At worst you'll fight with me. But that's okay. One does not take offence when one's children get angry."

That remains to be seen.

"What's the matter Amit? Why are you so quiet? You haven't spoken a word since I came in."

What should I say? Once you've delivered your intricate, finely crafted pieces, I will answer you with one rough but telling blow. It takes just one stroke of the blacksmith's hammer to equal the hundred delicate taps of the goldsmith's.

"I've heard that your new play has been held up."

Don't you worry about my play ... just get on with yours. This prologue has been stretched beyond boredom.

"I know you are proud and, to tell you the truth, I admire you for it."

Excuse me, but please be bold enough to use the right word. Don't say admire, say it's extremely painful. For all your wealth, it is pathetic to see how poor you are in terms of courage. Really, I pity you.

"Son, even pride must have a limit."

Which you have come to set, perhaps.

"The biggest problem is that Parul is no less proud."

Oh, so you're here to defend Parul's pride. Do carry on. As her mother you're fully entitled to ... Why the silence? You can't summon the courage or is it your good breeding coming in the way once more? Allow me to put it into words for you. Hear me out and feel free to correct me if I get it wrong. I won't mind at all. The thoughts will be yours, the words mine ...

It was after working with Parul for two years and getting to know her well that you married her, and that too of your own free will.

So tell me, how's that for a start? What sort of an actor would I be if I couldn't mimic your style? Let me continue ...

With such enthusiasm she set up house! So readily she took upon herself the financial and familial responsibilities of your home, just so that you would be free to devote yourself wholly to the stage.

Hey listen, even if you can't applaud, at least nod your head appreciatively. Perhaps your daughter's sorrows are upsetting you. All right, I'll cut it short ...

Having received these favours, one would expect you to realise how much you owe my daughter. But you are such a thankless fellow – I'll change that to "wretch" if you like – that you are replacing her with a new heroine in your play! Not just that. You have also insulted my daughter by flirting openly with your heroine and the other tramps of the stage. How dare you behave in this manner?

So tell me, this is what you came to say, isn't it? Perhaps also to issue an ultimatum – Such behaviour will not be tolerated any further! Either you will have to mend your ways or I will take my daughter back – and gladly too. It is not as if she were a waif with nowhere to go ...

Well, listen carefully!

The heroine of my new play shall be Nanda, since I feel she has tremendous potential which I intend to fully exploit. As a director, it is my duty to bring new talent to the fore, to foster it. And if Parul, in spite of her close connection with the stage, does not understand this aspect of the director's responsibilities and looks upon it as merely an excuse, then I'm afraid nothing can be done about it. You should see how devoted Nanda is at the rehearsals. She obeys my every instruction as though it were a vedic injunction. Respect for me oozes out of her every pore. She would do anything for me. Why then should I not take her?

Why do you look so upset, Ammaji? Oh, I see. You're wondering how I can compare the plain and simple Nanda with Parul and her winning combination of beauty, brains and character. They are as unequal a pair as Raja Bhoj and Gangu Teli. Nanda is a lightweight in every respect ...

I agree. But I also want you to understand how much substance this admittedly "lightweight" Nanda lends to my personality. Her very prescence makes me brim over with self-confidence. While with Parul ... let's leave it. You won't be able to take it.

Amit waited in vain for her to launch her bitter tirade, so that he could retaliate with his well-rehearsed rejoinders. But when Amma finally broke the silence and spoke, the tone was not what he had expected.

"Look, you married Parul ..."

Just married her. Didn't commit myself to lifelong slavery.

"To me, you are both my children ..."

Your darling daughter's life has been ruined.

"You, and even Parul, consider me an outsider. Just think, since Parul's father passed away, the four flats, two offices and whatever else there is belongs to the two of you. But apart from the pay she gets from the office, Parul will not accept a single paisa from me. She is putting aside two hundred rupees every month in order to build you a terrace theatre."

A terrace theatre! But I will only be doing street plays now.

"Your play is stalled for want of a little money but you two don't even mention it to me! And when I do find out, Parul makes me swear not to speak to you about it. All right, I know that you have your self-respect. But this money belongs to you. So where's the question of self-respect? Why this reluctance? Now, I shall not say nor hear another word. Just get on with your play."

Without pausing for a comma, she said her piece and threw down a bundle of notes tied in a kerchief. In one swift motion she rose and went clattering down the stairs, leaving Amit in a state of shock.

Amit felt his whole body tremble as his blood came to the boil. Oh, so he was to be defeated by this most base and low-down trick, presented in the garb of generosity. Having pushed him all the way into the mire of humiliation, she had walked away as spotless as a lotus leaf. He felt like shredding the bundle of notes to bits and throwing them at the retreating woman. But his blood, so recently boiling, had suddenly turned to water. His identity, his manhood, his very humanness seemed to melt and drain away, leaving him limp and lifeless. Wracked by an indescribably hellish pain, he knew he had to free himself from it soon. Or it would finish him off even as he sat there. Finish him for ever.

Freedom! In a flash Nanda's image was before him. In the past few months she had ceased to be a mere individual for him. She was his symbol of salvation. Whenever Parul's unspoken words flayed him and stripped him of his confidence, it was to Nanda that he would turn. Nanda, ever eager to please, whose every mannerism acted as a salve for his invisible wounds. He would come alive, a complete man once more. Nanda, only Nanda, could rid him of this agony. The very thought of her sent a shiver of excitement coursing through his lifeless body. How had he not realised that to these two women he was only a jester, funny and pathetic. No more. He would show them.

He would play the hero now.

Driven by a vindictive resolve, he snatched up the bundle of notes and thrust it into his pocket. Today he would do away with all restraints and inhibitions. He would use "his" money (that's what it would be in Nanda's eyes at least) to book a room in a posh hotel, and "order" the fanciest and most expensive food for dinner. And then, at his "masterful" best, he would enjoy Nanda. Thus would he confirm the reality of his existence and threatened manhood. How critical this had become for him today ...

And he rushed down the steps, eager to step into the hero's role.

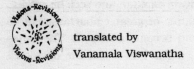

translated by
Vanamala Viswanatha

KUBI AND IYALA

by Poornachandra Tejasvi

"I have explained everything to him. You don't have to say a word. Just show him this bottle of medicine and listen to whatever he says," said Bayamma, coaxing her daughter Iyala.

"Appa has bought the medicine that the daaktar said. So why should I see him again?" Iyala protested.

Bayamma was irritated by her arguments. "You silly girl, Kubi daaktar is like a god. He only has to see you and touch the medicine bottle with his hands and all your aches will go away. Why don't you listen to me? Go now."

Iyala started for Bhairapura, a can full of milk in one hand and the medicine bottle in the other.

Iyala's father, Obrin, was a copy-clerk in Vittalaraya's estate. To supplement his income he kept a few buffaloes and every day Iyala delivered the milk to Subba Bhatta's hotel in Bhairapura. Today she also had to go to the Bhairapura hospital to show the medicine bottle to Dr. Kubera, or Kubi daaktar, and seek his advice.

The reason for this was a matter of great embarrassment to Iyala. Just the other day, she had become a woman. The aches and pains had been unbearable. If she had to tell the doctor all about it, she would never have agreed to see him. And that was what her mother had tried to reassure her about. But all the way to Bhairapura, one question nagged Iyala – What if the doctor had forgotten and she had to explain her problem? What would she do?

When Subba Bhatta saw the bottle in her hand he asked, "Who's this medicine for, Iyali?" "My mother is not well," she lied, her face red. Bhatta smiled, amused at the way she blushed. Iyala quickly emptied the milk can and went towards the hospital.

A smell unique to hospitals – a mixture of dettol, phenyl, and spirit – emanated from the building. The patients sat on a bench, waiting. Some were coughing, others discussing their ailments. An old man sat there gasping and wheezing. His grandson took his walking stick and was trying to balance it on his palm. Every time it fell down, he would pick it up and say, "Ajja, look this time," and start all over again.

The doctor was examining his patients in the room opposite. He took them to the inner room only if they had to undress. Iyala sat quietly at one end of the bench, watching Kubi doctor. When the doctor told the patient to say "Aah," the man opened his mouth like a hippopotamus. When the doctor said, "Say Eee," he bared his teeth. Putting the stethoscope to his chest, the doctor asked him to take a deep breath. The man made a sound like a snake! To avoid his bad breath, the doctor held his head slightly away and peeped into the cavernous mouth. Then he thumped the man on the back as he would a drum.

For Dr. Kubi, this was a routine matter. But Iyala watched him fascinated. Those serene eyes behind the glasses, the stethoscope garland round his neck, the solemnity with which he was advising the patients, made Iyala think that Kubi doctor was not just "god-like" as her mother had said. He was Jesus Christ himself!

Now it was the old man's turn to be examined. Standing up, he shouted for his grandson, "Elo, rascal, where are you? Here, give me my stick." The boy, carried away by his balancing act, had walked out of the hospital gate! The old man abused him loudly, and said, "I will never bring you to the hospital again." He snatched the walking-stick from the boy and hobbled into the consulting room. The doctor was waiting for him, a smile on his face.

Dr. Kubi examined all the patients, one by one – those who had minor surgery, those who were injured, those with coughs, running noses ... And so it went on for almost two hours. But there was no sign of exhaustion or impatience on his face. Rama Rao, who was preparing the prescriptions in the next room, was chatting with the patients ... He cursed those who had not brought a bottle, and ordered them to come later for the next dose. Into their well-like mouths, he poured different coloured liquids or threw in tablets as if he was tossing garbage into a dust bin. When one man screwed up his face at the taste of the medicine, Rama Rao sarcastically asked him, "What were you expecting, arrack?"

Iyala kept sitting. Even those who came after her had had their turn. As they left, her heart thudded with nervousness. She wished Compounder Rama Rao would go too. Dr. Kubi looked out and saw Iyala sitting there. The sunlight streaming in through the window made her curly hair shine. He motioned to her to come in. Rama Rao, looking out of his counter-window asked impatiently, "Who is that? Oh, Bayamma's daughter Iyali? Why don't you tell daktaar what the trouble is and take some medicine?" Iyala was shattered. So Amma had not explained anything. She lied to me! thought Iyala. Hesitantly, she walked into the doctor's room, and held out the bottle.

"Is this your medicine?"

"Yes."

"I'd prescribed it yesterday."

"Yes. Appa bought it."

"Did he manage to buy it here?"

"No, from Hassan."

"Take one teaspoon three times a day. You'll be all right."

"Amma said you should check it once."

"It's the right one. You can go now."

"She said you must give it to me with your own hands."

Kubi turned pale. This had happened too often. He had been trying very hard to fight the people's blind faith in him. But compounder Rama Rao, in a way, encouraged it. Instead of telling them about Kubi's knowledge, skill and dedication, he kept praising the strength in Dr. Kubi's touch and his superhuman power in curing disease. As a result, Dr. Kubera came to be equated with a Panjurli, or a wrestler!

Kubi called Iyala to his side and told her in a gentle voice, "Look Iyala, if the medicine is good, it will work. No matter who touches it, or who gives it. It makes no difference whether I touch it or not." Kubi was always careful with young girls. They came to him eager for reassurance. But he only had to speak to them kindly and they would attribute all sorts of meanings to his words. Yet today, irritated by Iyala's simple-minded faith in him, Kubi had called the little beauty close to him and had spoken with so much feeling.

Iyala stood there for a moment, overcome by shyness and humiliation. The doctor had refused her request. Tears welled up in her eyes. She turned away.

Rama Rao was watching them. "Saar, they really believe in your healing touch. Give her the medicine with your own hands. They won't wear out if you do."

"How often have I told you not to say these things, Rama Rao?" Kubi said sharply. "A disease is cured by the medicine. It does not matter who touches it. We are deceiving the villagers by doing this. I am not getting a salary for spreading such lies."

"Whatever you might say saar, a lot depends on the doctor. There was one Doctor Kalappa here. Poor man! No matter what he prescribed, not a single patient survived. If medicine is all that mattered, anyone could give it. You might say there is nothing special

---

Panjurli: a powerful spirit

in your hands. But that is only your modesty."

Kubi was quite disheartened by Rama Rao's logic. Yet he did not want to be cruel for the sake of his beliefs. He called out to Iyala. She looked at him, tears rolling down her cheeks.

"Iyala, today I'll give you the medicine with my own hands. But listen carefully to what I'm saying. Giving the right medicine is important. It doesn't matter who touches it. Believe me. It is the truth." Saying this, he took the medicine bottle and gave it back to her. He felt extremely uncomfortable doing something he had no faith in. And sad too.

Iyala, her head bowed, took the bottle and went away. Rama Rao watched it all as if it was a puja ritual.

D r. Kubi's full name was V.S. Kuberanath. He was a doctor in the government hospital at Bhairapura, a godforsaken place. Though it was the most important village in the taluk, its poor transport facilities and its almost non-existent trade, made it appear to belong to the Stone Age. Kubi, a competent doctor and a skilled surgeon, was forced by circumstances to come to this remote village.

When the war started, Kubi had joined the army medical service. By the time he completed his training the war was over. He was relieved. But soon, Kubi found that his hands which could work miracles in surgery when challenged, had very little to do. After all, only healthy young men are recruited to the army. At the most, they may have a cough or a cold, a pimple or a boil. Those who wanted to avoid drill, came to him on some pretext or other. That's how soldiers are! The result was that Kubi had no choice but to give up the army. Many people thought he had quit because he could not stand the rigours of army life.

When Kubi came back, the face of the country's public life had changed. Unemployment plagued the nation. Thousands of medical graduates were without jobs. Kubi was given this post at the Bhairapura hospital solely because he had served in the army.

Besides, no one opted to come to this wilderness, with an annual rainfall of more than 300 inches.

Since there had been no doctor in Bhairapura for so long, the compounder, Rama Rao, had been playing doctor. He had quite nonchalantly distributed medicines, tablets, even surgical instruments to the unsuspecting public. Kubi had to recover them from the cycle shop, the jeweller's mart, and the barber shop! Dr. Kubi was confronted by many things, not just disease. He had serious differences with Rama Rao, who would prepare an injection without sterilizing the syringe. Sterilizing surgical instruments was something he'd seen only during his training and he believed water was boiled at the hospital to make tea. He considered all the precautions and fuss about sterilizing to be the new doctor's superstitions. Hadn't the few doctors who had been here for a short time, fleeced their patients by injecting ordinary distilled water? Many of them had even been cured by it! Rama Rao handed out medicines that the patients wanted and sent the serious cases to the hospital at Hassan without the doctor's knowledge. Not only that, he started a whispering campaign to malign Dr. Kubi. One day, before Kubi reached the hospital, Rama Rao had, in one sitting, pulled out anything that looked like a tooth, from an old woman's mouth. The patient, a diabetic, lost so much blood that she nearly died. Kubi had to use all his knowledge and skill to save her. It was his army training and self-control that had prevented him from punishing Rama Rao severely.

This same Rama Rao had a change of heart one day. It was indeed extraordinary how it happened. That day, Rama Rao had an unbearable headache, so he popped some tablets into his mouth. Barely had he swallowed them, when his lips and eyes became swollen and gasping for breath, he collapsed. He was probably allergic to the tablets. He was unconscious for some time, hovering between life and death. Had Dr. Kubi not been there, he would most certainly have attained his heavenly abode that day. Kubi nursed him night and day, and brought him back to life.

Since then, Rama Rao had a great regard for and faith in Dr. Kubi. He became extremely respectful and loyal to him. Rama Rao had started telling every one he had seen Lord Krishna himself work through the doctor's hands the day the doctor had nursed him back from a half-dead state. Kubera scolded him for this, but Rama Rao insisted that he was not lying. Because, he said, no ordinary mortal could have saved him when he lay there lifeless for over two days and nights. "You may say what you like. I know what the truth is, so why should I worry?"

Such foolish talk often made Kubera seriously wonder whether a patient was actually cured by medicine or by faith. Any other doctor would have given up in frustration. But Kubi stayed on, determined not to betray either medical science or the physical world governed by logic and reason. He did not believe that he had any superhuman power or skill. Nor could he tolerate anyone who thought so. As a doctor he witnessed, every day, the terrible tragedies that resulted from such beliefs. This world of ignorance, which defied logic, was like hell to Kubi. He soon realized that if he wanted to fight disease, he had to first fight ignorance, the backwardness and superstitions that resulted from it, but most important, the cause of these evils, poverty.

Kubi's selfless efforts to combat all these earned him a good name and soon it became a household word. He was respected not only for his skill and sincerity, but also because after he came there, he had managed to get funds from the Taluk Board to repair the main road to Bhairapura. But how quickly attitudes changed – from a patient's normal confidence in the doctor to a blind faith in his touch!

These two things worked in tandem to aggravate Kubi's problem. Whether it is a hereditary characteristic of knowledge – to carry ignorance with it, or whether it is a historical irony – who knows!

If Rama Rao's former antagonism had been unwelcome to Kubi, so was his present faith and trust. Both were equally unfounded.

As Kubi's fame spread rapidly and diseases were on the decline, superstition and blind faith in him grew, subtly and imperceptibly, but with the same speed. That is why when Iyala asked him to touch her medicine, Kubi was so disturbed.

Two patients were waiting for Kubi when he came to the hospital that evening. One was a coffee plantation worker from Ummatthuru. His son had a swollen nose and a problem with his breathing. When the doctor asked him what he had done about it, the man said that he had taken a vow to appease the spirit, Otthuga.

Kubi examined the boy's nose carefully. It smelt like a dead rat. As he wiped it with dettol, tiny white maggots fell out. Bhairapura was a veritable treasure house of disease, thought Kubi. He cleaned the boy's nose thoroughly, gave him some antibiotics and sent him off. But Kubi was puzzled. How could maggots have bred in the nose? "It's all his karma, saar! Has anyone heard of worms in the nose!" Rama Rao stated. "It is God's leela. How else can you explain the presence of worms in the wild fig," he asked. Once, a friend of his had smelled a flower, and the worms in it ate up his nose ... He went on and on, distracting Kubi who was deep in thought. Suddenly, Kubi looked as if he had found the answer to a difficult riddle. "Look Rama Rao, your karma and all that is nonsense. This is probably what happened – the boy had a running nose. When he inhaled, along with the mucus, he must have drawn in some of the maggot eggs left on his upper lip. The body temperature was right for them to hatch inside his nose." The doctor's explanation was so convincing that Rama Rao wondered if Kubi was a trikaalagnani.

In the meantime, Bayamma had come asking for Iyala. Rama Rao told her that she had seen the doctor and gone. "She hasn't come home yet," muttered Bayamma as she went off in the direction of Subba Bhatta's hotel. No one paid any attention to her.

---

trikaalagnani: one who has knowledge of past, present and future

Just as Bayamma left, two coolies, Rehaman and Ranga, came in grinning. The previous day, they had been beaten by the police who were investigating a theft. The police knew quite well that these two were not thieves. But somebody had to be beaten up to show that they were doing their job. This had happened once before and Kubi, unable to tolerate the injustice, had gone to Inspector Asghar and asked him, "Why do you punish these innocent people?" To which the Inspector had given some nonsensical reply, "What to do, sir, big people lodge a complaint and we cannot ignore it. So to show some progress has been made in the investigation ..." Kubi had retorted, "But by your punishment, you leave them unfit to carry loads on their backs. What else can they do except steal?" And Asghar had calmly replied "Doctor, you have your problems and I have mine. If they go round saying their livelihood is threatened, then everyone will think I am an Inspector to take note of."

Kubi was distressed at the plight of the coolies. He removed the bandages and looked over the wounds on their backs. With great concern he asked them what had happened. Hearing his sympathetic tone, the coolies broke down. "There was no theft, swami. Where would we hide hundreds of sacks? The director and the secretary of the Society together have swallowed them up. Now, to mislead the people, they have lodged a false complaint against us. Whenever there is a theft in Bhairapura, this is what happens. We do not have so much money that we can bribe the police, swami!" they said tearfully.

Kubi had tried very hard to keep within the limits of his professional duties, but it was becoming impossible. Now, he had reached the end of his patience. He told the coolies that he would prepare a report of the police atrocities on them, and they could submit it to the higher authorities. "No, no, swami," they pleaded. "We hear our names are on their records as regular offenders. If they come to know we have complained, we'll be beaten up more. Just give us some good medicine that will heal our wounds fast." They added, "May your stomach always remain cool, swami."

Kubera cleaned the coolies' wounds, and seeing that they were healing well, sent the two men away without any bandages.

It had taken Kubi a long time to understand the heart-rending nature of Bhairapura's politics. There were two powerful rival groups, the Vokkaligas and the Lingayats. A few influential Muslim and Brahmin opportunists tied themselves to the tail of the winning bull. Whether it was for the control of the Society, the Co-operative Bank, or the Taluk Board, the conflict between them made life intolerable for everyone. Anything that came into contact with these politicking leaders was robbed of its truth and justice, and its true nature was completely distorted. Murder became an act of mercy, and theft a most noble duty while falsehood was transformed into truth.

When the coolies had gone, Rama Rao said, "It doesn't look like any more patients will come. Shall we close for the day, saar?"

Kubera did not hear Rama Rao. He was lost in thought. How could he prevent these frequent atrocities on the coolies? They had been the ones to be rounded up and beaten when Chukumal set fire to his shop in order to cheat the Bank. And then, when Maregowda had accidentally killed his wife and buried her secretly in the forest, it was the coolies who had been beaten up. Kubera had treated their wounds along with those of the four beggars who had put up their tents in the market-place, and of tailor Ramaiah who was suspected to be the paramour of Maregowda's wife.

The brilliant doctor's mind, which could diagnose and cure the most mysterious of diseases, suddenly grew numb. It was Rama Rao addressing him again, that brought Kubi back to the present. The compounder had already closed all the windows.

As Kuberanath was about to leave for the hospital the next morning, he received some ghastly news. A boy from Bhatta's hotel ran up to him and without pausing for breath, blurted,

"Daaktar, daaktar, somebody has killed Iyali. Rama Rao and Bayamma sent me to tell you. They have gone there."

For a moment, Kubi's face showed shock. But he was not easily shaken by death and suffering. One of the first lessons he had to learn in his profession was to keep calm in an emergency or a crisis. Kubi had achieved this control with considerable penance. Quickly regaining his composure, he asked "Where did it happen?" The boy replied, "Near the rock at the turning next to the dhoop tree. I'll show you if you wish." Kubi knew the spot well, and so declined the offer. The boy, hoping to get away from his chores at the hotel, walked back dejectedly.

When Kubi reached the spot, a big crowd had gathered there. Bayamma and Obrin were beating their breasts and wailing. A bus had come to a halt at an awkward angle, off the road. It had hit a pot-hole and the axle had broken like a flimsy toy. Bayamma's bawling found a sympathetic audience in the stranded passengers.

The crowd became quiet when they saw the doctor approaching. One man whispered, "This is Kubi daaktar! His touch can bring the dead back to life. Huvappa's daughter-in-law wanted to jump into a well because of unbearable stomach pain. I believe she was cured with just one dose of this great soul's medicine." "That may be so. But no one can bring this girl back to life, not even Brahma himself. They've slit her throat ..." commented another.

Swiftly, the doctor made his way through the crowd towards the body. The murder must have been committed the previous day. The smell of blood had attracted swarms of flies. The throat was partially slashed, the thigh bone was broken, the legs and skirt were stained with blood. It looked like a case of rape. The doctor quietly examined everything. There was a strange, un-human calm on his face. He had a quick word with Rama Rao, and then he started making notes of his observations. The crowd that was expecting an instant cure, or a miracle, broke into a chatter, disappointed by the sight of the doctor merely writing something.

The conductor of the unfortunate bus walked up to the driver.

"Anna, shouldn't you have driven more carefully? Look where you've landed me now – guarding a corpse."

"You guard it if you want. As for me, driving the bus to this village again is out of the question. This is the fourth time the axle has broken. Sons-of-bitches, they've only made a show of repairing the road. How will I face our sahukar, Shankar? If the bus keeps losing one axle a month and a tyre every week, how can he afford to pay us? Why does this wretched place need a road or a bus? Should set fire to this pack of scoundrels and their damned village."

Some people expressed grief over the fate of the bus. One of them began to abuse Sattar Sabu. "That sod Sattar Sabu has swallowed twelve thousand rupees sanctioned for this kanthratu, damn him. If a pregnant woman travels on this road, she will deliver in an instant." Another agreed. "Yes. You're right. Every one of them is a cut-throat rascal."

All of them knew the background and story to this road. The villagers blamed Sattar Sabu. He accused them since he was yet to receive two thousand rupees of the twelve sanctioned for the construction of the road. This was to be paid by the people of the village. Sattar Sabu had got the Taluk Board to certify that the people had paid their share. They, however, were dodging him. First they said they would pay him in cash after the harvest. Then they said they would give him an equivalent amount in the form of paddy. However, they went back on their word and gave neither. But they signed the statement that the work on the road was completed, so that Sattar Sabu could collect his money. Each time Sattar Sabu demanded payment from them, they threatened to report that the work was not satisfactory. In retaliation, Sattar Sabu had deliberately left a huge rock where it was, obstructing the drain near the dhoop tree. The rock could only be dislodged by blasting it with dynamite. After a great struggle with the Taluk Board, Kubi had arranged to have it removed.

---

kanthratu: a mispronunciation of contract, and a pun on the word meaning scheming or wily.

To Kubi that rock was a symbol of the backwardness of the village. The people, however, were not particularly keen on getting rid of it. They had even created myths about an eagle that nested there.

The people of Bhairapura had developed an inexplicable animosity for the new road. Once it was constructed, the Deputy Commissioner from Hassan and other officials started coming regularly to the village to recover loans, to collect levy paddy ... People seeking donations for dubious charities saw the new road and took a diversion. Visits of relatives increased. The consumption of coffee and milk shot up in every household. Excise police and goondas supported by the liquor contractor Venkatasetty regularly raided those suspected of brewing illicit liquor. Along with distilling equipment, they confiscated whatever they could lay their hands on. Squads to prevent black-marketing in coffee forced merchants to open their godowns.

In the meanwhile, the rainy season had set in. The gushing rain water, obstructed by the rock, began to flow onto the road. The gravel on the surface was washed away. The iron wheels of the bullock carts going to and fro made deep ruts which soon filled with water, making the road unfit for motor vehicles. The shuttle bus had to go to the garage every time it plied this route. Sattar Sabu had only trimmed the palm trees instead of uprooting them. Now they started sprouting blithely in the middle of the road. Big stones, used by drivers to prevent their vehicles from sliding back when they stopped there, lay strewn all along the road.

Kubi realised that there was no alternative but to get rid of the rock near the dhoop tree. So he had approached the engineers and the Chairman of the Taluk Board. No one in Bhairapura wanted that rock removed, but not one of them said so to Kubi. Among themselves they'd say, "Where do we have cars or jeeps? If we have a path for our bullock-carts, that's enough."

It was because of all these things Kubi was able to find the site of the murder without any difficulty.

Kubi had seen many cases of death and murder and poisoning. He always sent thorough and objective reports of his findings. The judges and lawyers respected his word in the court.

Now he examined the body cursorily. Telling Rama Rao to see that it was sent for a detailed examination after the police had recorded the statements of all concerned, he started walking back to the hospital. Several bus passengers and some passers-by accompanied him. One man began to recount whatever he knew about the murder ...

When Iyala did not come home, Bayamma went looking for her. Not finding her in the village, she went to her sister's house in Gubbagadde hoping Iyala was there. In the meantime Aravara Sesa, the cart man, had found the lid of Iyala's milk can. He recognised it and gave it to Obrin. It was he, Obrin, and two others, who had discovered Iyala's body ...

Kubi paid little attention to the man's voice droning away like a budabudkya's. Right now, he had to establish whether Iyala's death was a case of murder or rape. Bayamma had told him that the girl had had heavy bleeding and cramps. That was what made it so baffling. Let's see what the post mortem report says, he thought. I'll find out as much of the truth as I can within the scope of my profession.

Kubi had never cared for detective work, but he did have a feel for it. Whether he liked it or not, his job was similar to that of a detective's. Studying the nature and features of a disease, its symptoms, the patient's history, collating the observations in order to make a diagnosis, and then prescribing the right medicine – wasn't it detective work? But Kubi possessed the one trait that makes a detective different from a doctor. His sole aim was not to

---

budabudkya: a soothsayer

identify a thief, a criminal or a murderer and send him to the gallows. In the course of his career, he had seen many deaths and great suffering for which no man was responsible. People became prey to deadly diseases, and succumbed to them in spite of his tireless efforts. In the face of this "punishment without trial" Kubi did not think pursuing, nabbing and hanging a criminal was an act of great valour. And yet Kubi viewed Iyala's death from his own personal angle. Through it, would he be able to go one step farther in understanding this world, he wondered.

In the evening, Compounder Rama Rao came to the hospital dragging his tired feet. He told Kubi what had happened during the day. Iyala had been murdered inside one Ramanna Gowda's estate. Rama Rao, Obrin, Vittalaraya, the estate manager and the Superintendent of Police from Hassan – had all gone there. The police were interrogating everyone who had passed that way and noting their names and addresses.

"Who knows what misfortune awaits each one of us, saar? Out of a feeling of disgust, I told them, the doctor has already done what had to be done. Nothing more is going to be gained by cutting open the stomach. It is not a "poison" case. Why do we need a detailed post-mortem? Who wants that mess, that nuisance, saar? I wouldn't wish this fate even on my worst enemy. Which bastard could have done something like this, saar? Such a gem of a girl! What kind of case do you think this is, saar ..." Before he could finish, Kubi snapped at him, "Rama Rao, had I not asked you to bring the body for a detailed post-mortem? Who is going to answer the questions in the court, you or I? If you say it's not necessary, those police fellows will be even more casual about the investigations."

"No, no, saar! They won't be! They are going to bring police dogs, I hear. Also, a special CID squad is being posted in Bhairapura." With this explanation, Rama Rao slunk away as if he were dodging the swinging stick.

---

swinging stick: a Kannada proverb that says if you can dodge the swinging stick you will live a hundred years.

In the end, Kubera's fears were justified. Police Inspector Asghar took over the case saying, "The doctor has already examined the body and made out his report. What more is he going to say? Now it is our responsibility." The lesser the doctor's involvement, the easier it would be for him to manipulate the investigations.

As if he were doing a great favour Ramanna Gowda added, "Poor thing! She has suffered enough in life. Let us leave her alone in death. Just hand over the body, Inspector." The poor parents were moved by this show of concern. They were deeply distressed at the thought of receiving Iyala's body in a gunny sack, like a shapeless mass of flesh. So, using Vittalaraya's influence with the Inspector, Obrin took charge of the body. Iyala was buried with proper Christian rites. The little angel's soul became one with the past.

Following this incident, Kubera was caught in an indescribable turmoil. He was struggling not to let his mind swerve from his purpose and his duty. He discussed the doubts, suspicions, theories on Iyala's murder that Rama Rao often expressed. At first, Rama Rao said the cowherds must have done it. But they never grazed the cattle there. Besides, all of them were little boys, not old enough to commit sexual assault. Every time the subject of rape came up, Kubi felt guilty that he had not conducted a detailed examination. Rama Rao's suspicion shifted to the mad men in the market-place at Bhairapura. The whole village knew them. No one had ever seen them carrying any weapons, nor had they shown signs of violent behaviour. But Kubi was not certain that they were incapable of rape. Their minds were unsound but their bodies were healthy. Being deprived of a normal life they could be led to perverse acts. He told Rama Rao that they needed to be watched closely. Kubi invariably gave a new perspective and a different dimension to Rama Rao's thoughts and ideas.

The police at first pretended to be very understanding by handing over Iyala's body without a post-mortem. They took a bribe of fifteen rupees for it, though. As for their investigation, they got hold of people not even remotely connected with the case, and beat them up every now and then.

About this time, the elections for the Bhairapura Land Development Bank were held. The Vokkaligas saw to it that not a single Lingayat – Shivanna, Veerappa, Basavaiah, Gururaya – nor planter Pinto or Sattar Sabu, was elected. They had bought off most of the voters, while some had been taken away and brought back only after the elections were over. Once again the rivalry between the groups surfaced.

Shivanna, Gururaya, and Basavaiah approached Obrin through planter Pinto, because both were Christians. Pinto told Obrin, "What has happened has happened. Your daughter is gone. No point lamenting her death. Now help us to teach these Gowdas a lesson. Say that your daughter had a relationship with Ramanna Gowda. That Gowda has so much arrogance!"

They took Obrin to church and made him promise that he would give such a statement. That Obrin should be tempted by a little money and agree to this scheme, did not seem right to Bayamma. She could not bear to think of her dead child's name being disgraced. So the same evening she went to Lakshmidevamma, Ramanna Gowda's wife and told her everything. Ramanna Gowda was in a fix. His rivals had bought over Inspector Asghar, through Sattar Sabu. There was only one person he could approach – Kubi.

Ramanna Gowda sent a message to Kubi saying that he was very ill and the doctor must come and see him at once. Kubi went to the Gowda's house with his stethoscope and his leather bag.

On the way there, he saw two strangers sitting by the rock. One was a small boy. The other, small-made but older, was smoking a bidi. They stared intently at the doctor. Kubi did not recognise either of them.

When Kubi reached the house, Ramanna Gowda had just finished his bath. There was not a trace of illness on his face. Kubi was surprised.

"Daaktar-re," Ramanna Gowda said, "I need a big favour from you. I would have come there myself but these days people gossip about whatever I do. That's why I had to call you here."

"What is it?" Kubi asked brusquely. From the way Ramanna Gowda spoke, Kubi guessed it must have something to do with Iyala's murder. Everything mysterious seemed to be linked to it.

"It's like this – my rivals, the bastards, are trying to get Obrin to lodge a complaint against me, alleging that I had an affair with his daughter and to hush it up, I had her murdered. Am I a monster or what? Would I fool around with an infant? Daktaar-re, please certify that the girl had not come of age, even if she had. I will take care of the rest. I am planning to meet the Inspector-General of Police with our M.L.A.," Ramanna Gowda said, in one breath.

Kubi was thoroughly disgusted. Because of this dirty politics, attention was diverted from the real murderer. Everyone was being misled.

"Ramanna Gowda, did you murder Iyala?"

"What are you saying, daktaar-re? You also suspect me? It seems you are taken in by those Lingayats. This is not a good time for me, that is the truth."

"Just answer my question. Did you have her murdered?"

Ramanna Gowda was taken aback by Kubi's curtness. "Cheh! I had nothing to do with it. If you are suspicious of me, what can I do, tell me?" he said, a worried man.

"So you had nothing to do with it. Then just keep quiet. The matter ends. Why are you getting anxious? It is not so easy to frame charges based on lies."

"Ayyo daaktar-re, you don't know their secret plan. They know I am contesting the coming Taluk Board elections. So they want to blacken my name. That's all. But no one, not even their grandfathers can file a case and put handcuffs on me. I can get away with committing any number of murders. They are no match for us. It is all politics, only politics."

Kubi was utterly dejected. "Let me go Gowda-re. I'm not a political animal. I must go to the hospital – there is a lot of work," he said, picking up his stethoscope and bag.

Seeing that his scheme to draw Kubi into the vicious world of local politics had failed, Ramanna Gowda apologised. "I'm sorry I had to trouble you. You see, these Lingayats are jealous of us. Once we were their servants, now we are walking with our heads up. But you won't understand all this."

As he went down the front steps, Kubi said, "Gowda-re, if you get agitated by their attempts to point suspicion at you, what will it indicate? Think about it," and walked away briskly.

Kubi did not see the two strangers sitting by the rock. They must be the CID police he thought. It did not occur to him that they may be even remotely connected with the murder. When he arrived at the hospital, Rama Rao said that some facts on the mad men had come to light. They were, in truth not mad and were married with wives and children.

The people of Bhairapura gradually came to terms with the murder of young Iyala. At first, the news received little attention. After all, she did not belong to any powerful caste group in the village. But when planter Pinto, Sattar Sabu, Shivanna, Ramanna Gowda, Chandre Gowda, and others got involved, everybody became more interested in it.

Stories spread rapidly. There were rumours that police dogs were going to be brought in. These dogs were imported from some foreign country. In minutes, they could detect thieves and murderers. As soon as they saw a thief, they would chase him and bite him! So the people said. For one reason or other, almost everyone was alarmed. They discussed it in Bhatta's hotel. "It is not possible to say how a dog's mind will work, saar. What if, being unable to differentiate between murder and distilling illicit liquor, it attacks all of us? The police will celebrate!"

"The day the dogs are expected, I will make a dignified exit beyond the ghats. Let them go to hell!".

"How will they know which man is decent, which one is a scoundrel?"

Several such questions were asked.

One evening, an unfamiliar dog came charging towards a small group of people. They ran for their lives. Later they learned that it was a stray which a village dog had been chasing.

The same day, there was news that the cart driver, Arvara Sesa was absconding and the police were looking for him. Everyone was surprised. "Look at the son of a whore! A married man like him, he should not have had such ideas," said some. They assumed that he was the murderer. Kubi could not understand why Sesa had run away. Had someone paid him to murder the girl? Was he scared of the police? A brisk search for the missing Sesa went on.

Compounder Rama Rao came up to Kubi. "All kinds of stories are floating around, saar. Aravara Sesa's wife Bulli has been wailing that the police have taken away her husband. The people too suspect this. But they're too scared to speak up. Those low caste people can be brutes, saar. They're capable of destroying the entire village without finding out who is guilty or what is the crime. They will attack any house they can. Iyala's father Obrin is also missing. They say that Ramanna Gowda and Vittalaraya have kept him in hiding in Kerala. Who knows, it seems like this is a bad time ..."

He stopped in the middle of what he was saying, as a loud explosion shook the earth. Kubera turned to Rama Rao with questioning eyes. Rama Rao, equally surprised, looked at the patients. But no one knew what it was. Somebody was heard muttering, "Must be an earthquake." Kubera went back to his routine of getting patients to open their mouths, pressing stomachs and tapping backs.

In the evening, a man who came for his medicine, said that two men had arrived to blast the rock near the dhoop tree with dynamite. That morning, they had succeeded with only one portion of it. The rest of that huge rock did not look like it would surrender to the explosive. Kubi guessed that the two strangers he'd seen near the rock on his way to Ramanna Gowda's house were these men. He was happy that finally the rock was going to be out of the way.

When Kubi reached the hospital the next morning, the first faces he saw were the ones he least wanted to see – Rehaman and Ranga. Somehow, they taunted Kubi's sense of right and wrong. He addressed them first. "Why have you come? I've taken off your bandages. The wounds must heal on their own. There's no need for any medicine."

"No, swami. This time we need a favour from you," they said walking with Kubi towards the consulting room. Kubi wished a fearful epidemic would wipe out this whole village, its people and their problems!

"We've been called to the police station again today, swami. You only tell us, what have we got to do with that murdered girl?" asked Rehaman.

This question was almost like a profound philosophical enigma to Kubi. He hadn't written the post-mortem report yet.

"What can I do, Rehaman? I am not sure any more of who has what to do with whom or why! When they beat you, it is supposed to be a warning to the others. If they beat you, it is only to get their salaries! Tell me, how can I help you in this situation? I can only stitch up your wounds and put ointment on them to make them heal quickly," Kubi said, mocking at his own helplessness.

At that moment, a terrible sound was heard – similar to the one heard the previous day. This time, neither the doctor nor the coolies were startled. They knew what it was.

Sorrowfully, the coolies looked up at Kubi. "Swami, then do us one last favour. You're like the God who gave us life. Tell the Inspector. Let them peel off our skin if they wish. Let them beat us anywhere else. But let them not touch our backs," they pleaded with tears in their eyes.

Kubera's mind was trapped in a terrible turmoil. His professional discipline, restraint, patience were all in conflict. As if to rescue him from himself, there was a sudden commotion in the street. Kubi had opened his mouth to speak, but the words did not come out. A man ran up to him. "The two men who had come to blast the rock are injured in an explosion," he said. There was chaos in the hospital. Everyone clamoured to know what had happened. The coolies did not think it was right for them to go on with their woes. They went away, trembling with fear at the thought of the police station. Telling the patients that he had to attend to an emergency, Kubi packed his bag and left for the site of the blast.

Kubi understood the seriousness of the accident when he reached the spot. A sharp quartz splinter had severed the hand of the younger man and he was bleeding profusely. As Kubi was trying to prevent a further loss of blood, the man, already unconscious, breathed his last. Kubi was surprised. He looked carefully for the cause of death, and found that another splinter had split the man's skull and penetrated his brain. His long thick hair had concealed the wound.

The other man looked all right at first sight. Actually, most of his body had been scorched. When Kubi reached his side, he was slowly regaining consciousness. Carefully they moved him to the hospital. Seeing his condition, the other patients forgot their own illnesses. Strangely, his face didn't show any signs of injury or suffering.

Rama Rao managed to get a detailed report of the accident from him. The previous day, the men had bored two holes in the rock and planted the dynamite sticks in them. They ignited one. It exploded. Then they lit the second one. They waited for a long time, but nothing happened. Thinking the fire had died down, they went away. Many people had passed that way. Some had stopped to chat near the rock. Others had even sat on it.

The next morning the men returned and started boring another hole next to the earlier one. They had worked with dynamite for so long that they thought they were immune to it. There must have been some life left in the fuse and their hammering sparked it off. Before they knew it, the rock had exploded. The dynamite they were carrying in their pockets intensified the blast. The older man's back and more than half his body was burnt.

While Kubi was attending to his injuries, he discovered that the man had several venereal diseases. Not that it mattered now, for Kubi did not expect him to live. However, as he lay on the hospital bed, covered with a sheet, he looked quite normal.

As more and more details about the accident came to light, people became less and less sympathetic. "Mad bastards. If you play with fire, what else do you expect?" criticised some. Others who had sat chatting near the rock, were shocked. "Careless fools, is this what they wanted to do to us? It is God's mercy. He taught these rascals a lesson!" And they sang of the glories of God and of the rock. For they had seen a certain logic in the way the rock had behaved. If there are dogs that detect thieves, why not rocks?

Inspector Asghar prepared his report after taking statements from everyone concerned. But he was not particularly interested in the case. It did not involve any bigwigs.

When the coolies reached the police station, Inspector Asghar was not there. He had gone to investigate the blast tragedy. His deputy Nanjappa shouted at them. "You rascals! If, in a fit of anger, we give you a few lashes, you carry tales to that Kubi daaktar and then dance to his tune? We'll wipe you out from the face of this village, wait and see. The director of the Society, the master who gave you food, you dare to tell stories about him?"

Shivanna, the director of the Society, was afraid that the two coolies would reveal how he had misappropriated the Society funds. Several times, when he was diverting stocks to the black market, it was they who had loaded the truck. He had also got them to adulterate the fertiliser by mixing sand from Kadur with it. That was why Shivanna had kept a close watch on them. He was planning to get them implicated in some case or other and then have them hanged. Or by using threats and harassment, force them to run away from the village. When Kubi doctor started taking interest in them, he was alarmed. He had also heard that the coolies were going around saying, "The daaktar is going to report everything to the authorities." Actually, the coolies were quite ignorant of all his misdeeds. They had mixed the sand thinking that it was some chemical manure!

Iyala's murder was most opportune for Shivanna. Just when he was planning to meet Inspector Asghar about this matter, Aravara Sesa and writer Obrin had disappeared one after the other. This was an additional ray of hope for Shivanna. He told Asghar to summon the coolies and have them severely beaten. He would then intervene with a show of sympathy. After that it would be quite simple to pay them some money and make them leave the village.

The reason for Shivanna's anxiety was the huge amount of money embezzled from the Society – nearly seventeen lakhs. Who had swallowed it, who knows? When Shivanna had started looting the Society, anyone and everyone had grabbed what they could. The only way Shivanna could keep his loot was to either make someone disappear by killing them or by forcing them to run away. Then, accuse them of misappropriating the funds.

Perhaps no one, other than Kubi doctor, had the moral right to save the coolies.

As they came out of the station, Ranga said, "Rehamananna, Asghar Sabu might spare you because of your caste. But for me, there's no chance." Rehaman did not say anything. He too was worried. Both of them were beginning to realize that they were merely sacrificial goats in an affair entirely unconnected to them. They had made up their minds to run away from the village, knowing fully well that the moment they disappeared, they would be charged with Iyala's murder. But they had no choice. Before they could act, they wanted to consult Kubi doctor one last time, so they went towards the hospital.

When they reached there, it was almost dark. Kubi and Rama Rao were fully occupied, attending to Lory's burns. Both of them were sweating profusely as if they had done some strenuous work. Lory was hovering between life and death. They were injecting glucose-saline into Lory's blood. When Kubi noticed the coolies he motioned to them to go away quietly.

The next morning, the news was out that the coolies had disappeared. This time the whole of Bhairapura was surprised. Then there was another rumour that the Aravara community was planning a riot. All the hotels and shops started pulling down their shutters.

Shivanna congratulated the Inspector, "Good work! What did you do to them?"

"We have our methods. I can't tell you all that. You'd better see to it that that interfering daaktar doesn't report about me!" said the Inspector. He had decided to fleece Shivanna, so he didn't tell him that the coolies had run away on their own.

There was a reason why Kubi was preoccupied when the coolies had turned up to see him the previous evening. Lory had not thought that he would die of his burns. But as days went by, the burn blisters started oozing and with that, his life slowly started draining out. He was either delirious or unconscious most of the time. Before he went home that evening, Kubi told Rama Rao that he did not think Lory would live very much longer. Hearing this, Rama Rao began to make enquiries about Lory's relatives. Lory must have been conscious, then, and heard all this. Suddenly, he started howling that he had killed the Christian girl near the rock.

Rama Rao was stunned. He could not face this truth alone and he rushed to Kubi. They hurried back to the hospital, with some hope. But Lory had lost consciousness when they reached there.

Some serious questions stared at Kubi – Had Lory really confessed, or was Rama Rao imagining it? Had he really murdered

Iyala? Why had he done it? It seemed as if Lory would die and leave all these questions unanswered for ever.

Kubi had to make Lory speak one last time. For just one moment, he had to be freed from the clutches of Yamaraja, so he could answer a few questions. Kubi accepted Yama's challenge, undaunted, and resolutely set to work, equipped with an oxygen cylinder, glucose-saline and haemoglobin. Lory was almost dead. Rama Rao could not even feel a pulse. Kubi massaged his chest to keep his respiration going and injected coramine into him.

To Rama Rao, everything Kubi did that evening, seemed like the funeral rites a kapali would perform on dead bodies at the burial ground. His belief that Kubi was superhuman was further strengthened.

Around midnight, when the spirit is supposed to return to the dead body, the patient regained consciousness and started mumbling feebly. Kubi asked Rama Rao to find out what he was saying. Rama Rao shouted into Lory's ear, "Why did you kill the girl? Why?" Leaning over Lory's mouth, he waited for an answer. In the dead of night, in the silence of the hospital, Rama Rao's voice sounded disembodied and unearthly. Rama Rao kept repeating, "Yes. Tell me. Tell." Like a long-distance telephone call, thought Kubi. The gist of what Rama Rao gathered was this – Lory had believed that sexual intercourse with girls who hadn't attained puberty would cure venereal diseases.

"That's right. But why did you kill her?" Rama Rao persisted ominously. The patient slowly drifted into unconsciousness.

Kubi came out. It was pitch dark. Like a prophet, he thought about the days to come. Lory had committed this heinous act believing that sexual intercourse with Iyala would rid him of his venereal disease. Then, afraid that somebody might find out, he had killed her. Or probably because he was angry when he found that she had already come of age. Or in panic, when he saw her lying there unconscious, her thigh broken.

When this became known the next day, the coolies would be vindicated, and the whole village rid of an oppressive evil force. The people would give up one superstition to adopt another. The rock near the dhoop tree would remain where it was. It would now become a centre of pilgrimage.

I must warn the Inspector to leave the coolies alone, thought Kubi. I have managed to prevent my responsibilities from spreading beyond the bounds of my profession. But what have I achieved, he wondered.

By the next morning, the news of Lory's confession had spread like wild fire. Everything had happened too fast for Kubi's comprehension, but to the people of Bhairapura, it was clear as water.

Believing that the Inspector was responsible for Aravara Sesa's death, the Aravaras attacked the police station.

Lory had raped and murdered Iyala, the little angel. So she had her violent revenge the next day. Otherwise, why should the embers, sleeping the whole day, not harm anyone except these two men? Kubi Doctor had invoked Lory's ghost and learnt the truth. In the presence of the honest and truth-loving doctor, even ghosts, spirits and phantoms bowed their heads.

The people sang the praises of the rock and Kubi Doctor.

It is an irony of Fate and a mockery of Time that Kubi should become a symbol of everything he had disbelieved, fought against, rejected.

translated by
Vidya Pai

INNOCENCE

by Chandrakant Keni

S quatting in the shade of the cashew tree, Jayyu held the cashew fruit steady with the big toe of her right foot and began to peel it. Devu came and sat in front of her, his kashti full of fruit and nuts.

"Move away. The sap might get into your eyes," Jayyu warned him.

"Jayyu," Devu whispered, making no effort to get out of the way.

"What is it? What are you staring at? Didn't you hear what I just said?"

Devu paid no attention to her. "Jayyu, how is it that your thighs are so fair?"

Jayyu's dress had crept up when she sat, exposing her thighs. But she was not aware of it till Devu asked her this question.

She laughed. "You roam about all day wearing nothing but a kashti. That's why your thighs are burnt and dark."

"Then the rest of your body also must be so fair! Is it?"

Now Jayyu was embarrassed. She dropped the cashew and tugged at her dress, her face red.

"Will you let me touch your thigh, Jayyu?"

"Your hands are covered with sap."

"No, they aren't. I swear they are not. But I'll wash them in the spring if you like."

"But why do you want to touch my thigh?"

"Please, Jayyu. Once. Only once. Don't say no."

Without waiting for an answer, Devu placed his hand lightly on her left thigh and let it wander. Both of them felt a shiver run through their bodies. Jayyu shut her eyes. She felt a pleasant sensation, as though someone was gently stroking her body with a peacock feather. Devu felt like he had touched the sky.

Jayyu was about fourteen years old and Devu a couple of years younger. They had, for many years now, been coming to this hillock with their cattle. They would run around, pick wild fruit, play all sorts of games. Today Devu had come up with this new game.

"That's enough," Jayyu declared after a few moments. "Let's peel some more cashews."

"Let me touch the other thigh too. Please ... "

"No."

"Didn't you like it?"

"What?"

"Didn't you feel nice when I touched you?"

"No. And what did you get out of it?"

"I liked it."

"You've gone mad," Jayyu spluttered. "Come on. Let's finish peeling the fruit. God knows where the cattle have strayed."

Devu withdrew his hand. Emptying his load of cashews, he too set about peeling them. Neither of them spoke as they worked. From time to time Jayyu would dart a quick glance at him. Suddenly a jet of sap squirted into Devu's eye. He rubbed it furiously with the little finger of his left hand.

"Aaah! It's burning. I hope I don't go blind," Devu whimpered as he stood up, still rubbing his eye.

Jayyu got up. "My hands are covered with sap. But wait," she said. Bunching the end of her dress, Jayyu blew hard on it. Then she fomented his eye with the warm cloth.

"It's still burning, Jayyu. What shall I do?" Devu wailed.

"Let's see if I can take it out ... Don't move," she said. Standing close to him, Jayyu ran the tip of her tongue lightly over and around Devu's eye.

The burning stopped. "Ah," Devu sighed in relief, closing his eyes.

All of a sudden, Jayyu pulled Devu close and pressed her lips tightly against his. For a moment their warm breaths mingled. Then she quickly pushed him aside.

"Cattle also show affection like this, don't they?"

Jayyu turned red. "Cattle don't have hands!"

"Shall we put our tongues into each other's mouths?"

"Our mouths? Won't they ..."

"We can wash them at the spring afterwards."

"No, baba. I'm scared."

"Scared of what?"

"All the women say, Be careful of men. If you go too close to them, you will become pregnant."

"How can you get pregnant if you are not married?"

"You can! Don't you know about Shevanthu, the beggar's daughter? She is not married, but she is pregnant. It seems she went too close to that fellow who drives the truck at the mine."

"How do you know all this?"

"I heard the women talking about it at the well yesterday."

"Let's get married!"

"Married? But you are only a child. A husband must be old. He must be working. The women are looking for a bridegroom for me."

"Who is he?"

"How do I know?"

"Will you go to your husband's house then?"

"I'll have to ..."

"And I'll be left all alone here?"

"You too will get married one day."

"But can I get a bride like you?"

"What do you mean, like me?"

"With fair thighs."

"All women have fair thighs."

"Really?"

"Of course."

"Jayyu, will you really leave me here and go to your husband's house?"

"All girls have to go."

"Let's run away."

"Run away and go where?"

"I don't know. I am confused. My head's spinning."

"Your head's spinning because you are scared. See how late it is. Get up. Let's go home."

Reluctantly, Devu walked down the slope with Jayyu. His mind was in a whirl. Jayyu spoke to him twice, but he did not answer. When they reached the foot of the hillock, she stopped.

"Are you angry with me, Devu?"

"No I am not. I swear."

"Why are you so quiet, then?"

"Will you really go to your husband's house, Jayyu?"

"Look, Devu, you wanted to put your tongue into my mouth, didn't you? Come. Let's go under that banyan tree ..."

"No. I don't want to anymore."

"Why?"

"You'll be someone else's wife."

"So?"

"Jayyu, don't go. Don't go to your husband's house."

"We'll see about that when the time comes. Why think about it now?"

Jayyu took his hand in hers. At that moment, like a dam that had burst, Devu began to cry. Drawing him close, Jayyu wiped his tears with the end of her dress and patted him comfortingly. Resting his head against her, he cried for a while. Gradually he calmed down. Waves of contentment seemed to wash over him ...

The moment was shattered by a piercing whistle.

"Very affectionate you two are getting!" taunted Santan, the toddy tapper, from his perch atop a palm tree.

Devu looked sheepish. Jayyu ran away.

translated by
CPA Vasudevan

I have had many unusual experiences in my life. The incident of the Blue Light is one such. Rather than call it an amazing experience, I should describe it as a bubble of mystery, which I have tried to prick with the pin of scientific enquiry, but have not been able to. Maybe you can. Maybe you can even analyse and explain it.

I refer to it as an amazing experience because ... well, what else can I call it?

This is what happened.

The exact date is of no consequence really. It was the time when I was house-hunting every other day, because I never seemed to find a room or house I really liked. The place I was living in had so many faults, but who could I complain to? "Don't like it? Then leave it" is what I'd probably be told. Leave and go where? So I stayed, unwillingly, reluctantly, till it became unbearable. Then the search would begin once more. I

THE BLUE LIGHT

by Vaikom Muhammad Basheer

was fed up. How many houses, how many rooms, had I lived in, and hated. It wasn't anybody's fault. I didn't like the place, so I moved out. Someone else who liked it, moved in. That's the way it is, I suppose, with all rented houses. But these days, houses to let are in short supply. And the rents! What you could have got for ten is not available for even sixty today. Anyway ...

I was wandering around on my quest for a dwelling when suddenly, there it was – a house, with an ancient signboard saying, HOUSE TO LET. It was a small, two-storey bungalow, standing beside the public road, far away from the bustle and the noise of the town, but within the municipal limits. I liked it instantly. It was an old house, rather dilapidated and neglected. I didn't care. It was good enough to live in. Two rooms and a portico above, four rooms below, bathroom and kitchen, water connections, but no electricity. Just outside the kitchen was an old well with a stone parapet around it. The toilet stood in one corner of the compound. There were lots of trees. A compound wall enclosed the whole place. Fortunately there were no other buildings nearby.

I wondered why no one had grabbed it yet. It was like a beautiful woman, I thought, one you would want to shield from public view or hide behind a purdah. I was excited, and also afraid I might lose it. So I ran around trying to collect money for the advance. I borrowed enough to pay two months' rent, took the keys and quickly moved in, occupying the upper floor. The same day, I bought a hurricane lantern and some kerosene oil.

A great deal of garbage had accumulated all over the house. I cleaned the whole place myself, sweeping and mopping the rooms upstairs, the ones on the ground floor, the kitchen, the bathroom. What a lot of dust and rubbish! I went over it all a second time, thoroughly scrubbing the floor. That done, I had a bath. I felt very pleased. In this state of mind I went and sat on the parapet of the old well. How delightful this place was! Here I could sit and dream. Or run about the compound. I would plant a garden in front, roses mostly, and some jasmine. Should I hire a cook? No, that would be a headache. I could go out after a bath for my morning tea and bring some back in my thermos flask. Lunch would be at a restaurant. Perhaps they would agree to send my dinner home. I also had to meet the postman, tell him my new address and warn him not to give it to anyone.

I could look forward to some lovely nights of solitude. Days too. I could write and write and write.

All these thoughts were racing through my mind as I sat there, gazing into the well. It was so overgrown with weeds that you couldn't tell if there was any water in it. Without thinking, I picked up a stone and dropped it into the depths. Bhloom! it went. Yes, there was water in the well.

I was feeling a little tired. I had not slept a wink the previous night because so many things had to be done. First, I had to settle my account at the eating house. Then meet the landlord and tell him I was moving out. After that, I had to pack. I bundled up my folding canvas cot, carefully put away my gramophone and records and tied them firmly together. Then I got my trunks, easy chair, shelf and all my belongings ready for transport. At the crack of dawn I had brought them to my new house.

I looked at my watch. Eleven o'clock. I was hungry, so I decided to go and find an eating place. I locked the front door, put the key in my pocket and shut the gate. As I stepped out on to the road, I thought to myself, With whose song, with which record, shall I inaugurate my new residence to-night? I have over a hundred records in English, Arabic, Hindi, Urdu, Tamil and Bengali. None, as you can see, in Malayalam. We do have talented Malayali singers and their records are available, but the compositions are not very good. A few new composers are coming up. I must buy some of their work. But tonight, whose song shall I play – Pankaj Mullick, Dilip Kumar Roy, Saigal, Bing Crosby, Paul Robeson, Abdul Karim Khan, Kanan Devi, Kumari Manju Dasgupta, Khurshid, Juthika Ray,

M.S.Subbulakshmi ... Finally one comes to mind, *Door desh ka rahnewala aayaa* – "The man from a distant land has arrived." Who had sung that song? A man or a woman? Never mind. I would find out later.

Just then I met the postman. I told him of my change of residence. When he heard the new address, he was shocked.

"Ayyo saar! An unnatural death took place in that house. No one can live there. That is why it has been vacant for so long," he exclaimed. I was a bit rattled.

"What unnatural death?"

"You know that well in the compound? Someone jumped into it and died. Since then, the place has been haunted. Many people tried living there, but they found the doors kept banging at night and water taps were mysteriously opened."

Doors bang? Taps open by themselves? Strange. I recalled noticing that the taps had locks on them. The owner had told me it was to prevent trespassers from jumping the walls for a free bath. It had not occurred to me to ask why the tap inside the bathroom had a lock on it too.

The postman went on, "It catches you by the throat, saar! Didn't anyone tell you all this?"

A fine dilemma I was in. I had paid two months rent in advance and now ...

In front of him, I put on a brave face. "That's all right. I only need one of my mantrams. You just make sure my letters are sent there."

Although I said this quite bravely, I am not really a brave man. But I'm not a coward either. I just fear all those things that most people are afraid of. Very well, let us say I am a coward for I do not go seeking unusual experiences. But if one comes unsought? What would happen? What should I do in this situation? As I walked along, my stride grew slower.

I entered a restaurant and ordered a cup of tea. My appetite for a proper meal had been replaced by a burning in the pit of my stomach. I spoke to the owner about sending my meals to the house. He saw the address and said, "I will send all your day-time meals. But at night, none of my boys will agree to go there. A woman jumped to her death in that well. She may still be hanging around." He looked at me again. "Aren't you afraid of ghosts, saar?"

"No. I'm not," I replied casually. "I have my mantram."

I kept talking about this mantram. What mantram? I didn't know either.

Hearing that the ghost was a woman, half my fear had evaporated and I was somewhat reassured. She must have some traces of tenderness still left in her, I told myself.

I had my tea, made arrangements for my food and then walked to the bank nearby where a couple of my friends were employed as clerks. I told them of my predicament and they promptly berated me.

"That was a very foolish thing to do. Couldn't you have asked us before you took the house? We would have advised you. The place is haunted. And it is men who are attacked by the ghost," they said.

So, it is men she hates.

"Who knew all this at that time? Anyway, why did the woman jump into the well?"

"Love. All for love," one of them said. "Bhargavi was her name. She was twenty-one years old, had just finished her B.A. and had fallen passionately in love with this man. But the fellow went and married someone else. On his wedding night Bhargavi jumped in the well and died."

So that is why she hates men.

By this time most of my fear had gone.

Confidently, I told them, "Bhargavi won't bother me."

"Why won't she bother you?"

"My mantram, my mantram."

"We shall see. Soon you will be screaming for help."

I chose not to reply.

A little later I returned to the house. I opened the doors and windows. Then I went out to the well and called out softly, "Bhargavikutty!" After a few moments, I began ...

"Bhargavikutty, we don't know each other. Let me tell you about myself. I am the new tenant here. I consider myself a very decent man. A confirmed bachelor. You know, Bhargavikutty, I have heard people make so many complaints about you. You won't let anyone live here in peace ... You bang doors in the middle of the night. You open up the water taps. You put your hands around men's throats and strangle them ... That's what I've heard. Now, tell me, Bhargavikutty, what do you want me to do? I have paid two months rent in advance, and I can't afford to let it go. I don't have pots of money. Besides, I like this house of yours very much. It is your own house, isn't it?

"I want to work here in peace and quiet. I write stories, Bhargavikutty. Tell me, do you like stories? If you do, I shall read all my stories out to you ... We have no quarrel with each other, do we? There is no reason for any. Oh yes! That stone I threw into your well. That was quite thoughtless of me. Forgive me. It will not happen again. Bhargavikutty, do you like music? I have a fine gramophone and a couple of hundred first class records ..."

I stopped. Who was I talking to? This well, with its gaping mouth, waiting to swallow anything that is thrown into it? The trees? The house, the air, the sky, the world ... to whom? Or is it to my own troubled mind? No, I said. It is to an abstraction that I speak. To Bhargavi, whom I have never seen. A young woman of twenty-one. She loved a man. Dreamt of living as his wife, his lifetime companion. That dream remained a dream. Despair seized her. And disgrace ...

"Bhargavikutty," I said, "you need not have done this. Don't think I am criticising you. True, the man you cared for did not love you. He married another. Your life was full of bitterness. But you must forget the past. For you, there will never be another disappointment."

"I am not finding fault with you, Bhargavikutty, but tell me honestly, did you die for the sake of love? Love is the Golden Dawn of Eternal Life. You didn't know much about that did you, you foolish girl? At least that's what your animosity to all men proves. Let us say, for argument's sake, you loved a man. He wronged you. Even so, is it right to see all men in the same light? Had you lived longer, had you not taken your own life, you would have found that you were mistaken. There would have been another who loved you, who called you his goddess and worshipped you. But as I said earlier, you will never have such an experience. For you history will not be repeated ... Bhargavikutty, how will I ever get to know your story?"

I paused for a while. Then in a placating tone, I continued, "Anyway, you must not trouble me, Bhargavikutty. This is not an order, it is only an entreaty. If you were to strangle me tonight, no one would come looking for revenge. Not that such a thing as revenge is possible in your case! What I mean is, there is no one to do it. You know why? Because I have no one to call my own."

"I hope you understand, now that you know everything. Both of us have to live here. Yes. I propose to stay. In the eyes of the law, this house, this well, they are all in my possession. But ignore that. We are going to share it. You may use all the rooms downstairs and the well. The kitchen and bathroom, we'll go fifty-fifty. Do you approve of the arrangement?"

I waited for an answer. Nothing happened. But I felt a sense of relief.

Night fell. After a meal at the restaurant I came home with my thermos full of tea. I lit the lantern by the light of my torch. The room was bathed in yellow light. I went downstairs. It was dark. I opened the windows, and stood there for a long time. Then through the kitchen to the well I went, intending to lock up the taps. But I changed my mind.

Coming inside, I shut and bolted the door, climbed the stairs to my room and poured myself some tea. I lit a bidi, and sat in the easy chair, preparing myself to start writing. I felt someone was standing behind my chair.

"I do not like people peering over my shoulder when I write, Bhargavikutty," I said, and turned around.

There was no one there.

The mood to write was lost. Instead, I felt a strange restlessness, and began to pace up and down. Outside, the air was still. Not a leaf stirred. I glanced out of the window and suddenly, for the briefest moment I saw a light. Blue? Red? Yellow? I don't really know. It was only for a moment. Had I seen it, or was it my imagination? I wondered. But you can't imagine something like that. Must have been a firefly I saw.

I stood by the window for some time. Nothing happened. I tried to read but could not concentrate. I thought I would play one of my records. I lit the lantern again, opened the gramophone, fitted a new needle, wound it up. The world was silent, but there was a humming sound in my ears. Was I scared? A strange feeling crawled over my back. This silence was oppressive. I needed to shatter it into a million fragments. Who would do that for me? Which song would it be? After a brief search I picked out a record of the Black American singer, Paul Robeson. His deep baritone sang out, "Joshua fight the battle of Jericho."

After that it was Pankaj Mullick with *Tu dar na zara bhi* – "Do not be even a little afraid!" Then the enchanting *Katrinilay varum geetam* – "Wafting on the breeze comes the song," by M.S. Subbulakshmi. Slowly, I began to feel at peace with myself. I had Saigal himself sing in that gentle, comforting voice of his, *So jaa rajakumari, so jaa* – "Go to sleep, my princess, go to sleep."

"That's all for now, Bhargavikutty. Tomorrow there will be more," I called out, as I closed the gramophone, lit a bidi, extinguished the light and lay down. By my side were the torch and my watch. The door to the portico was shut.

It was around ten o'clock. There was silence all around, but for the ticking of the watch. I lay with my ears strained. There was no fear in my mind, only a sort of calm watchfulness. It was a familiar feeling. I had known it in different places, in the different lands that I had travelled, during the twenty-odd years of my solitary existence. I have had experiences whose meaning I have never been able to comprehend. My thoughts kept shuttling between past and present. But at the back of my mind, I was waiting. Is the door about to bang? Was that the sound of water flowing? Will her hands? Such thoughts kept me awake until three in the morning. All this while I heard nothing, felt nothing, experienced nothing. Not even dreams.

It was nine in the morning when I woke up. Nothing had happened!

"Good morning, Bhargavikutty!" I called out cheerily. "Many thanks! Now I know you are being maligned. But let them say whatever they want, eh?"

Many days and nights went by. Bhargavi was always on my mind – her mother, father, brothers, sisters – whose stories I did not yet know. Most nights I wrote. And when I grew tired of writing, I played my records. Before each record I would announce the name of the singer and explain the meaning of the song. "Listen. This is by the great Bengali singer, Pankaj Mullick. It is a sad song about old times. Listen carefully."

Guzar gayaa woh zamaanaa, kaise, kaise.

Or, "This is Bing Crosby's In the Moonlight which means ... Oh, forgive me. I forgot you have a B.A. degree."

And so I would carry on this conversation, all by myself.

Two months and a half went by. During this time, I had completed a short novel. I had even laid out a garden and announced that when the flowers came, they would all be Bhargavikutty's. My friends visited me, and sometimes they even spent the night at my house. On such occasions, before going to bed I would quietly slip downstairs and speak into the darkness.

"Listen, Bhargavikutty. My friends are here tonight. Don't strangle them. If something like that happens, the police will come and take me away. So take care. Good night!"

Whenever I went out, I would tell her, "Bhargavikutty, look after the house. If a thief breaks in, feel free to strangle him. Only don't leave the body here. Carry it off and throw it three miles away. Otherwise we'll be in trouble." If I returned home late after a night show I would always call out from the front door, "It's only me, Bhargavikutty!"

All this, let me admit, came out of the initial excitement and novelty of living in a haunted house. As the days wore on, however, Bhargavi faded from memory. There were no more long monologues. Only an occasional mental glance in her direction.

Let me explain why this happened. From the beginning of the human race, countless men and women have died on this earth, have they not? All of them have dissolved in the waters or gone up in smoke or turned to dust – to rejoin the earth in one form or another. We all know that. In my mind, Bhargavi too had entered that category of beings. She had lapsed into memory.

That's when it happened.

I had been working on a story, a very powerful, emotional one, from nine o'clock in the night. I was writing furiously, when I noticed the light was getting dim. I picked up the lantern and shook it gently. No oil. I was too deeply involved with the story to stop now. I thought that I would write another page at least. I had done it before, writing in the fading light. So I raised the wick and continued. The light faded again. Up went the wick a second time, and a third, all four inches of it, until it turned into a mere glow. I switched on the torch, turned the wick of the lantern all the way down and, needless to say, the light went out. What could I do now? I had to have some oil for the lantern. It was after ten o'clock. Where could I get kerosene oil at this time of night? Ah yes! My bank friends used a kerosene stove. I could borrow some from them.

With torch and bottle, I left the room, shut and locked the door behind me, went down the stairs. I locked the front door and walked to the gate. Closing it behind me, I strode down the empty road. It was cloudy but there was a little moonlight. I walked fast.

When I reached the bank building, I called out to one of my friends. He came down and opened a side gate. I entered the compound, went to the rear of the building and climbed the stairs. I found three of them playing a game of cards. When I asked for the oil, they laughed.

"Why didn't you send your girlfriend Bhargavi? Have you finished writing her story?"

I did not reply. But in my mind I resolved that I would, indeed, write it. As one of my friends started to pour the oil out of his stove into my bottle, it began to rain.

"Now you will have to lend me an umbrella as well," I said.

"Umbrella? We don't have even a piece of an umbrella. Why don't you join in the game? You can go when it stops raining."

I sat down. Because of my carelessness my partner and I had to perform three salaams in forfeits. My mind was still on the story, and the cards did not get the attention they deserved.

Around one o'clock it stopped raining. I finished the game, picked up my torch and bottle and got ready to leave. My friends prepared to go to bed. When I reached the road they turned their lights off.

Not a soul stirred. The street was dark. In the dull moonlight, the whole world lay hidden behind an indistinct veil of mystery. I walked quickly in the direction of my house. What thoughts raced through my mind at that time, I do not know. Flashing my torch, I trod the silent, deserted road. Not a single living creature crossed my path.

Reaching the house, I opened the gate, walked up to the front door, entered it and bolted it behind me. There was no reason to suspect that anything unusual had happened. And yet, for no special reason, my mind was filled with a strange melancholy. Normally, I laugh easily but find it impossible to shed tears. Instead, a kind of compassion overcomes me. It came to me then and I felt that I must weep. In that emotional frame of mind I went up the stairs. A strange sight met my eyes.

When I had left the house my lantern had gone out for want of oil. The room lay in darkness. Since then, two or three hours had passed. It had also rained.

Now when I returned, I could see a light in the room through the crack in the door. It was a brilliant light that my eyes saw and my subconscious registered. My rational, conscious mind had not taken note of it yet. As usual, I took the key out of my pocket and flashed my torch on the lock. It shone like silver and it seemed to smile at me. I opened the door. Every fibre of my being was startled into awareness. A tremor shook my body. But it was not in fear that I shivered. It was a mixture of love and compassion. I stood there, still, speechless. I felt hot. I perspired. I wanted to cry.

The room, the white walls, everything, glowed in a blue light. A light from the lantern, burning with a two-inch tongue of blue flame.

Who had lit the lantern? Where had that blue light come from?

translated by
Padmaja Punde

S he stood by the window, alone and distracted. Dusk had just set in. Everything around her seemed forlorn. Brooding. A few stars in the sky ... A shapeless, odd-coloured cloud ... The horizon smudged by the pale twilight ... and in the distance, a mirage. Vehicles and human beings scurried about in the street. A tree, sensitive, withdrawn ... A quiet breeze, a gentle rustle ... Some specks of light ... From the womb of silence the whisper of nascent night.

He came into the room. She sensed his presence and turned around.

"What's this? Why are you standing in the dark?" he asked.

"Just ..." she mumbled.

The usual evasive reply. Should I go up to her and ask ... he wondered. But he knew it would be of no use. She wouldn't tell him anything.

He looked around, picked up a file and walked away. But as he

AND THEN A ... THOUSAND SUNS

by Vijaya Rajadhyaksha

went, he switched on the light. In its harsh and unfriendly glare, she withdrew further into her shell.

Coming in again, he asked, "When will dinner be ready?"

"It's ready."

"Serve me, then. I have some work to do early tomorrow morning."

"All right. I'll lay the table."

He followed her silently and sat down. Picking at the food disinterestedly, he glanced up at her. She was eating mechanically, her head lowered.

Dinner over, what next? Bed.

He lay down. After a while she came in and curled up beside him, knees drawn to her stomach. He was aware that she was rubbing her back, trying to turn to the other side, sighing imperceptibly now and then. She lay only a few inches away from him. But was it only a few inches, he wondered. She seemed to be far away, in some unknown land. Could he ever get there? It seemed impossible.

It was only a week ago ...

Waking up in the middle of the night, he had seen her, a shaft of light from the next building falling on her body. Her eyes were closed, but she had been tossing and turning, as she was now.

"What's the matter?" he had asked.

"Nothing."

"You won't tell me ..."

"Really, it's nothing."

In the early years of their marriage, whenever she had behaved this way, he had gently pulled her into his arms and her stubbornness had melted away. This time too he tried it. He touched her. But turning away, she implored, "Please don't." He was hurt by her tone. And angry.

"All right. As you wish," he replied curtly.

It had happened so often lately, ever since the seventh month of her pregnancy. Whenever he had tried to come close to her, she had moved away. Her youthful body in full bloom drew him to her. But she avoided him. Some nights she suggested, on others openly asked him not to touch her.

Why did it have to be this way?

Perhaps she doesn't feel like it in her advanced state. He could sense her discomfort. Her tossing and turning. Her aches and pains, her tensions. But how was he to know? She wouldn't tell him anything. Unable to relax, he would drift off to sleep, away from her.

During the day it was better. She wasn't as distant and even spoke to him sometimes, about their son Ajit, who was now with her parents, or about the little things he should do after she went to the hospital.

"Look," she would say, "if I feel uneasy during the day, I will go to the hospital immediately. I will phone you before going. But there's no need for you to rush. Don't worry. Everything will be all right." Her words amused him yet they were comforting. He felt relieved that she was so calm.

Why did she become a different person at night?

About a week ago she had taken down the suitcase from the top of the cupboard.

"What's all this?" he had asked in surprise.

"Let me keep it ready, just in case. I don't want any last minute rush. There is no one to run around, anyway."

He wondered if he had made a mistake. Perhaps he should have sent her to her parents'. But it was she who had insisted on staying back. Her mother had supported her. "One feels worried if it is the first time. Now everything should go smoothly. I'll take Ajit with me, though. That will give her some rest."

After a long time they were by themselves. But she was glum, lost in herself. He saw her hovering around the packed suitcase, looking preoccupied. He tried to comfort her. "Relax. There is plenty of time. Try to rest."

Reluctantly he would go to the office. Away from home, he worried about her. At home, he found her aloofness, her curt, monosyllabic replies oppressive. He felt trapped in her silence. Her delicate condition made it even more difficult for him to protest.

This was a new experience for him. The last time she had gone to her parents in the sixth month. It was just nine months after their marriage. They had shared an intense relationship, a constant togetherness. The first night, and then many similar nights. Occasionally, an afternoon brimming over with ecstasy. Soft words, caresses. He would arouse her. And she would open up to him. They would come together. Merge. Sometimes she pretended to sulk. He would gently woo her. Again, moments of intense passion. They immersed themselves in this experience.

She soon became aware of a life stirring within her. How emotional she was! "We must take care of you now" he would say as he gently took her in his arms. "Unh hn," she would reply. "What unh hn?" He was proud and haughty, but he was tender and gentle too. She had never moved away from him. Not even on the night before she went to her parents. The idea of giving birth to a baby did not frighten her then. She did not talk about strange, irrelevant things. She was dreamy, wistful.

Even after she went away, the memory of her fully bloomed body was deeply etched in his mind. The two months just flew. He often wondered, Will it be a girl? A boy? Not for a moment did he try to imagine what the baby would look like. In fact, he often wished that the baby would remain in her womb forever. Then she would always be like this, brimming over with joy and fulfillment.

One Sunday after she had gone, he wandered around, ate out, saw a movie and returned home happy and cheerful. He had received her letter the previous day. He intended to read it once again before going to sleep. Just as he lay down with it, the telegram arrived. She had given birth to a boy that morning. He was overwhelmed, he couldn't fathom his own feelings.

What was I doing then? Perhaps I was still asleep. Did she suffer a lot? Was someone with her? She had once said that they don't usually allow anyone inside. He had wondered why, but hadn't asked. Did she go through it all alone? Was I in her thoughts, then? He had heard that some women become hysterical and curse their husbands. Had she? How did she feel when it was all over and she saw the little one for the first time? Did she think of me?

A tumult of questions rose and subsided in a thousand images of her body ...

Her next letter had all the details. The pains had started at midnight. They couldn't get a taxi easily ... How scared her mother was. The doctor's casual, "It should be over by evening." How wrong he had been! Suddenly the pains had intensified, and the last half hour ...

He read it all. But it did not make much sense to him.

A month later, he went to her mother's house and saw Ajit for the first time. He asked her questions about Ajit's birth. She just smiled and said, "How can you ask me such things?"

"Why not?" he had said. "You are not a stranger. You are my wife."

"So what? One can't talk about some things."

"But you always did!"

"That was different. Besides, even if I told you, you men would never understand."

That day he felt that she had moved away from him. She was still cheerful, giving – willingly, generously. And yet ...

Her body was mature. Her waistline thicker, her bosom heavier. He remembered how her breasts had looked in the early days of their marriage. Small. Firm. When she was pregnant, they had grown and become fuller. Her stomach seemed to merge with her bosom. But she looked slim from behind. Now she was full all round. After the baby came, her breasts sagged, as did her stomach.

What had happened in the meantime, he wondered. She had dismissed his questions with, "How will you men understand?"

Why not?

Was he not meant to know?

What happens at that instant when a seed changes into a

sprout? Why the dome-like barrier around this one moment? Will the doors of that dome never be opened to a man? Could no one let him in? So many questions flashed through his mind. Where would he find the answers? He fell silent. Soon he forgot everything in her burgeoning body. She was eager, giving. Perhaps a trifle distant. But it didn't bother him.

She was different this time. Had the previous experience of childbirth frightened her? Was the thought of going through it all once again driving her into a shell? Probably. She had been all right during the first five, six months. It was only in the seventh month, after Ajit had been sent to her mother's house, that she had become so quiet.

"Do you miss Ajit?"

"Yes."

"Shall I bring him back?"

"No. He will be neglected here."

"Let us ask your mother to stay with us."

"For what?"

"You, all alone ..."

"So? This is not the first time. Why should we be scared?"

"But it's better if you have someone with you."

"You're there, aren't you?"

Strange replies. Was it anger? Resentment? About what?

Hadn't she wanted the second child? He could not remember her ever saying anything like that. Of one thing he was sure. This time she had not been as excited about the baby. On the contrary, she seemed upset. She had asked him once, "Shall I see a doctor?" He had wondered why. Once she realised the inevitability of the situation she was reconciled to it. But now this strange behaviour! He was exhausted trying to understand it. Finally he gave up. He became uncommunicative too. And angry.

The distance between them increased. The gap couldn't be bridged even at night. He lay alone, suffering silently.

Three months had passed. Not once had she come close to him. He would wake up in the middle of the night and stare at her sensuous body, luminous in the moonlight. Sinuous, dazzling like a snake. Her jet black hair, her smooth skin, her quicksilver eyes. Her imperfect nose setting off her round face perfectly. Her slightly thick lips. Her slender neck, shapely arms and those delicate fingers! He couldn't take his eyes off her. She had had a baby, yet she was graceful, fresh. Showering him with all this beauty, drenching him in it.

Is this body mine? To possess? To enjoy? Are all its curves, its undulations familiar to me? Have I been witness to all its changes? How did I first see it? Come to recognise it? Was I embarrassed? Was she?

I saw her for the first time four years ago. She was a stranger then. Sitting awkwardly, a little away from me. My eyes had registered the fair complexion, an oval face, expressive eyes, full lips curved charmingly. I had liked her immediately and said yes to the proposal.

After the engagement we went out together. Away from the crowd. Sometimes I would ask a question and she would reply. I wanted to establish to myself and to her that we shared a deeper relationship. So how should I behave? I was confused. Who knows what she felt. She seemed bewildered. I remember one evening ... the setting sun, the gentle breeze. She was walking silently beside me, keeping a respectable distance between us. Where I got the courage from, I don't know. I pulled her closer, held her hand, our fingers tightly interlocked. The touch made me bolder. My inhibitions forgotten, I hugged her, kissed her. Her soft luscious lips, long, curling eyelashes, her slightly warm breath, and her breasts crushed against me ... soft, small, firm. How I wished she had remained there a little longer ... But she moved away.

After this she became bolder. Began to talk about her family, her friends, herself. Very soon, she started teasing, scolding, sulking.

I too opened up.

We met regularly. At home, or outside. We wanted to talk, to share every little experience. And as we talked, we yearned to touch, to feel, to explore, to know each other more intimately. One day, I saw her from behind. The deep ravine of her arched back. Her sari worn low, barely concealing her seductive waist. I felt as if I knew her a little better.

On our wedding night she was standing with her back towards me, bashful, shy. After much persuasion, she slowly turned around and lay on the bed. Her body took a different shape. Breasts slightly flattened, fair, slim thighs, eyes half closed, warm breath, soft, shy voice. Eager, expectant, promising. That night, she confided in me, all her little secrets. What had happened to her one day when she was in the eighth standard. How terrified she had been! The time a boy in her college had tried to ... she had been furious. She went on chattering.

Finally I had asked, "Is that all?"

"Yes. I hadn't told anyone about it till now. I haven't hidden anything from you. I never will."

Yes. She hadn't kept anything from me now. I stroked her dishevelled hair, and she fell asleep. At peace.

I remembered ... how she adjusted her sari when she got up, rearranged her pallav, draped it neatly around her shoulders. How she gave herself. And withdrew. Like flashes of lightning, her body playing hide and seek with me.

In the early days of her pregnancy she lost weight, looked faded. Her eyes became dull. But barely three months later, she began to glow. She was excited. If someone asked her why she looked tired, she would look at me and smile mysteriously. I knew everything. She described to me the minute changes taking place in her body, uninhibitedly. Once I saw a couple of bluish veins clearly etched on her belly. They reminded me of a flash of lightning.

The life in her womb too was slowly taking shape. It throbbed and pulsated as it grew. And the shape of her abdomen changed according to its size. Mostly at night, and sometimes during the day, she would moan softly when the baby moved. If it happened when people were around and someone asked what the matter was, she would merely look at me and smile, a special smile. Yes. I knew everything. Even her heavy, languid gait.

Then something had happened. What? God alone knows.

After the delivery, she put on weight. Her bosom lost its shape. But she didn't care. Her blouse would remain unbuttoned. Her breasts would get wet. She would get cramps ... She would complain about Ajit ... Sometimes her breasts would become like stone ... and she was in agony.

But she told me everything.

Soon, her body regained some of its lost shape. The breasts shrank, the belly still sagged a little, the complexion was a shade darker, but she was as innocent and guileless as ever.

Had she changed a little?

As Ajit grew up, she became aloof. She stopped confiding in me. When a friend visited her, I no longer got a detailed account of their conversation. She threw away letters without showing them to me. When she felt unwell, she didn't tell me immediately, as she used to. Only if I noticed her looking listless and asked her what was wrong, she would come out with it. If a mention was made of pregnancy or childbirth, she'd say emphatically, "God, no! Not that experience ever again."

I would then try to probe, to find out more about it. She would be evasive or ignore my questions altogether.

She had certainly drifted away.

Why had I not sensed it sooner?

What had happened at that time?

Something certainly had. Her body bore marks of it. What was it? Why couldn't I understand? She refused to explain.

Now, the wonder once more. She blossomed again. Had I been witness to it all earlier? Had I experienced it before?

Not everything. Had she stayed back after the seventh month the last time, she would have shared it with me. She trusted me then. Now she deliberately keeps herself aloof.

Does the reason for it lie in that unravelled mystery that I don't understand?

He wanted to see it all. Once. Just once. Her fullness, her overflowing abundance. Those blue veins on her belly. Are they standing out now? And what else?

But she was far away, in mind and in body, deeply absorbed in herself. At times she lay with her back towards him, pretending to be asleep. Sometimes moaning or tossing and turning ... He knew she was awake. Near him, yet far away. Not a word was exchanged.

He was aroused. Excited. At night, wild desire ravaged him. That four-inch distance between them ... she had really stretched it out. Can't I snap it, regardless of her resistance, he wondered What will she do? Perhaps she is hoping for such aggression. But then her panic-stricken, Don't! came to mind, and he was ashamed of himself.

Why is all this happening to me? Why is my body so uncontrollable? The last time she was away for three months. The initial intoxication had not worn off. Haunted by her body, I had been restless. But not like this ...

One night he even said to her, "Why are you being so stubborn? Tell me. I can't bear it any longer."

"What can I tell you? It hurts."

"But just a little ..."

"Unh hn. Don't want anything."

Though he was furious, he didn't have the courage to persist. Desire continued to torment him.

One day he went to office as usual, but with a sense of foreboding. What if it happens today? There is no one with her. Will she go to the hospital alone? Will it be as bad as the last time? What if it is worse? If she can't bear it? Nothing terrible will happen, will it? All these fears rattled him. Sheepishly he went back home. She was surprised.

"What's the matter?" she asked.

"Not feeling too well."

He lay in bed the whole day.

Another day, he had just entered his office and sat down, when Sunanda Nadkarni walked in, bright, attractive, vivacious. She was an animated talker and he wanted to chat with her forever. To look at her, see her from all sides ... the curves, the undulations.

On the way home that day, visions of shapely forms and figures kept floating before his eyes. Some seen, others unseen yet familiar.

Shapely arms.

Fair feet.

An excruciatingly tiny waist.

He didn't feel guilty about it at all.

Was it a sin?

Of course not.

This frustration. She was responsible for it.

How proud she was of her body! As if only she has a body ...

Everyone has a body ... Every body guards a secret ... Each secret is shrouded in mystery ... But there is a chink in the shroud ... And every person is privy to the secret of at least one body ...

But is that true? Then why am I being barred from the secret of her body? The secret protected by a sky-vast dome, strong, impenetrable, like armour.

This dome destroys the relationship between one body and another. Separates them, not by a few inches, but miles.

One evening she asked, "Will you have dinner?"

"So early?"

"Yes. Let's finish it."

It didn't occur to him to ask why. He sat opposite her eating quietly. As he took a sip of water, he looked up. She was just picking at her food.

"What's the matter?"

"I am not feeling too well." She sounded miserable.

"But why didn't you tell me earlier?" he asked, concerned.

"I thought I'd wait a little. But now ..."

"That means ..."

"We have to go. That's why I said we'll have dinner early. As soon as I tidy up, we'll leave."

"Don't worry about all that. I'll tell the maid to do it."

His mind went blank. He couldn't move.

She plaited her hair, then went into the bathroom to wash her face, but took a long time coming out. Anxious, he started pacing up and down. When she came out, relief! She was wearing a dark coloured sari, had powdered her face, put kajal in her eyes. Just before leaving she lit a lamp in front of the family deities. Hands folded, eyes closed, she prayed. Opening the kuyri, the mango shaped silver case, she applied kunku on her forehead.

"Let's go," she said.

She was radiant. Alluring.

Calm. Composed.

How?

His voice trembled, "You come slowly. I'll get a taxi."

The taxi at the hospital gates. Midnight. Eerie silence. Everything at a virtual standstill.

The lights in the general ward were switched off. In the dim flickering shadows of the verandah, the tick-tock of the nurse's shoes could be heard. At the end of the corridor, to the left, was a row of special rooms. The Sister's room was further ahead. Beyond it, the labour room and the operation theatre. He was reading the name plates as he walked behind the nurse. She followed them slowly. Sometimes he would turn round and ask, "Are you all right?" Her replies didn't reach him. The nurse had spoken to him quite curtly, but she was kind and gentle with her.

"Walk very slowly, hn. I'll inform the Sister."

"Has the doctor come?" he asked anxiously.

"Yes. He's upstairs."

"Then ...?"

"Then what? Sister will examine her," was the nurse's brusque retort.

"Sister? But we wanted ..." he began angrily.

She silenced him with a pleading look.

"It's all right. It's too early to wake up the doctor."

He stared at her.

She and the nurse exchanged conspiratorial smiles.

What was all this about, he wondered.

When they reached the Sister's room, she sat down, leaned back and closed her eyes.

"Do you want to lie down?" the Sister asked her sounding a little worried.

She shook her head.

"Would you like some milk?"

"No," she said opening her eyes.

"When did the pains start?"

"In the evening."

"Is this the second baby?"

"Yes."

"How was it the first time?"

"Normal. But it took very long."

"How are the pains now?"

"So far, they were in the stomach. Now even in the back."

"Are you spotting?"

"Yes, since a little while."

"Come inside then."

He was listening carefully, curious. As she went in, she said to him, "Please wait here for me." He watched her as she entered the labour room. Suddenly she stopped and moaned softly, "Aai ..." The nurse supported her and said reassuringly, "Wait a moment. Don't be afraid. Sister is going to examine you. Everything will be all right." He felt like rushing up to her, to hold her close, to comfort her ... But she was going far away, into an unknown region where he was not allowed. He was left behind, alone.

Alone. On a deserted island, cut off from the rest of the world. Huge, menacing waves rose wildly around him. It was pitch dark. He could see nothing. Hear nothing. He was barely able to hold himself up. The island had no paths. No roads. There was just frightening emptiness. The waves engulfed him.

He was trapped. Alone. With only memories for company.

The wedding night. Then the second night. Yet another, vibrant and ecstatic.

Then one, colourless, unfulfilled.

Flowing tresses ... magenta sari ... blouse drying on the clothes-line ... pallav falling, exposing firm breasts ... fair thighs ...

The female form haunted him. Caused all the problem.

This form that will keep metamorphosing. Create newer forms. Treasuring within itself, seeds of generations to come. The female form, the creator. Intoxicated by its glory, it has dispensed with me.

He sat there, eyes closed, benumbed.

She entered the room. To him, it was like a flash of lightning on a dark cruel night. Startled, he staggered up.

"Did Sister examine you?"

"Yes."

"What did she say?"

"It's still early."

"How long will it take?"

"Can't say. Maybe by tomorrow morning ..."

The nurse came in. "Go to room number seven. Your bed is ready."

A tiny little room. Two cots. A dressing table. A jug of water, a glass. Curtains at the window and the door. The nurse pointed to a switch. "The bell is here. If you need anything, just ring it. I am right next door. Don't worry. Sister has given you a tablet. Soon you will feel sleepy."

As she left the room, the nurse addressed him, "You will be staying with her, won't you?"

"Is it all right? What should I do?" He was uncertain.

"Stay ... Yes. He will stay with me," she told the nurse feebly. The nurse went out.

He looked at her, surprised.

She seemed to be in pain. Her face was contorted. She gripped the bar of the cot, her body arched slightly.

"What is it?" he panicked.

"Nothing ... Just a spasm."

"Shall I ring the bell?"

"Don't ... This will go on for some time."

How would she go through all this? I may be here, but what can I do? She must bear the pains herself. A feeling of utter helplessness came over him. He sat next to her and started stroking her hair.

"I am sorry you have to go through this tension," she said.

"What tension? Don't be silly."

"Maybe I should have gone to Aai's. Then you would have been spared all this. She would have accompanied me. Last time, she stayed the whole night. I wouldn't let her go out for a minute. Not even when they took me inside ..."

"Shh! Don't talk so much. I will stay with you this time. All right?"

"Promise?"

"Yes. Promise."

She was getting tired with every spasm. At home, she used to say bravely, "I can go alone. It's no problem. After all, it is the second baby."

Where was that courage now?

"What time is it?"

"Ten-thirty," he said looking at his watch.

"Only ten-thirty? Oh god! Another five or six hours to go ... It will take long ... Why don't you lie down?"

She was becoming weaker. He had always been a weakling.

She clasped his hand tightly. Then let it go. Sometimes she would grab the railing of the cot. Her body would stiffen with every contraction, then relax. Again she said to him, "Go and rest. I'll soon be fast asleep."

To please her, he lay down. But his attention was on her, on her body, tensing, relaxing.

He was all alone, on a deserted island. For company, memories of a distant past, from his previous incarnation ...

This had happened before ...

It would happen again. And again.

A body was created. It grew up. Gave pleasure ... The body also gave pain ... It harboured a secret ... The secret was not shared ... So the body suffered alone. For millenniums.

Eternal pain. Everlasting ... So too the body.

The body splits. Then becomes one again.

Living in the shadow of Death, it is revitalized.

The mere thought of this miracle gives me goose-flesh.

Where do I figure in this drama? Why am I alone?

Will you ring the bell?" A voice pierced through the darkness. Quickly, he sat up and grabbed the bell switch.

"Is it very painful?"

"Hm! I don't think it will take long now."

"How do you know?"

Even in this condition she smiled at him. Then suddenly she grimaced. She was drenched in perspiration.

"I am very scared."

"Don't be afraid. I am with you. The nurse will be here in a minute."

The nurse came in. She mumbled something. The nurse said, "Then let's go. Can you walk? Or should I get a stretcher?"

"No, no. I'll walk."

Her voice betrayed her fear. Shivering and sweating, she leaned on the nurse's shoulder and walked with slow steps.

Now she will go in ... And I remain here?

Impulsively, he asked, "Can I come in with you?"

She looked at the nurse.

"We have no objection," the nurse replied.

He held her arm gently and walked beside her.

The labour room. A narrow cot with a thin mattress. A stool at the foot. She let go of his hand and with the nurse's help, lay down. Her body was taut. Occasionally, she whimpered. The nurse comforted her, "Relax. It's all right." Another nurse had come in. The Sister stood next to her. Sometimes she would hold the Sister's hand and look at her pleadingly.

He stood a little distance away from them, bewildered. He felt dizzy. He thought he was going deaf ...

Suddenly, she arched her body.

"Don't do that. You are making it harder for yourself," someone standing by her, scolded.

"Aai ... I can't bear it any more."

A loud, heart-rending cry ... Then deathly silence.

Again the cry ...

Screams.

The nurses in a flurry.

He realized what was happening, and tried to move forward. The Sister was saying, "The pains are not strong enough. That's why it's taking so long."

"Should we call the doctor?"

"It's not necessary. It's a straightforward case. The head is visible now. Another two or three contractions ... Only, they must come in quick succession."

He stepped back, and waited afraid even to breathe. Feeling, thinking ...

A dome ... Its doors closed ... Around the dome, a body jealously guarding it ... How fascinating this body! Ensnaring, rejecting ... The dome ... Far away ... Obscured in the body's mist ... Or lost in the body's radiance ... One body, bringing forth another ... Sound within a sound, word within a word, colour within a colour ... This body is the Real ... The ultimate truth ... It is sound, touch, form, flavour, fragrance ... All of these ... Variations of these ... So many manifestations of this body ... One a bud, the other fully bloomed ...

One open wide, the other tightly closed ... To savour this body is the true meaning of life ... To revel in it, the senses are inadequate ... When one is intent upon the pleasure it offers, one tends to forget the existence of the dome ...

In this lies the deficiency of the male body, and causes it to be alienated from the dome ... As if it had nothing to do with the dome.

Then comes one uncompromising moment. Images of the dome haunt you. Questions erupt.

Why am I outlawed? Why the guard?

Why am I so far from her body? And why are her experiences such a closely guarded secret?

But now the guard is becoming careless. The body wrestles with itself. One half disappears.

She used to fill the whole bed when she lay down ... This cot seems so empty now!

"Aai ... " A desperate cry.

Whose cry is it?

There's no one on the cot ... There is, a blurred shape ... semiconscious.

With the cry, a door opens slightly. The dome trembles. Quakes. The door opens wider. A roundish velvety mystery peeps out. Covered with light-as-froth down.

"Where is he?"

"She is calling you."

With the Sister's summons, he comes out of his daze. Tiptoeing up to her, he asks, "What is it?"

Her eyes are closed.

"Are you there?" she whispers.

"Yes. Right here."

"How long will I have to suffer? I have no energy left."

The Sister butts in, breaking the delicate bond, "I told you not to talk. Be quiet. Absolutely quiet."

He moves to the foot of the bed.

"Aai ..."

A huge wave rises and breaks. The circle becomes bigger.

"It's almost over. A couple of minutes more," the Sister sighs in relief.

The dome is spinning ... Fast ... Faster ... Circles ... Spheres ... Surf ... Foam ... Waves ... Some red, some snow-white ... A spray of water drenches him completely ... Wiping wet eyes what does he see? Hidden behind the clouds, a reflection of the sun ... Clear water below the moss ... A myriad images ... Colours ... Countless suns ... Refulgent ... No sky ... No space ... Nothing above, nothing below ... No Nature even ... Shapes, forms fuse ... The breeze blows, ripples rise ... The breeze stops, they fade ... Nothing else must emerge ... This moment is for the Bee. Let it come out of the lotus first.

Black as the bee, light as the foam, the down. Again the dazzle, the circular motion.

Death, deluge, forests, flames, lightning, spirits, fractured space, torrents, writhing serpents, all-devouring tongues, a grab, a swoop, a gulp.

The dome is still spinning, disappearing within its motion.

Taking with it the universe.

Only the Bee remains.

Aai ...

It is the bee calling out. It speaks with her voice. There's water everywhere. The bee moves. So delicately, so gently. As if it would slide out without splitting the lotus. The lotus picks up the rhythm and sways.

Aai ... Aai ...

"Sister, my mouth is dry. Some water ..."

"Here. Shall I go now? There's another patient waiting."

"No, Sister. Don't. Not yet."

"Very well. But don't be afraid. Its almost over."

"Aai ..."

The lotus hums Aai, Aai, Aai.

Suddenly, thunder. Then humming.

Opening. Closing.

Darkness. Lightning.

Eyes shut tight. Wide open, staring.

Floating images of frothy down.

In a split second, that life leaps out.

A wail. An intensely moving sound.

"A boy," the Sister announces.

He is overcome. Cannot remember anything, cannot see anything, cannot feel anything.

Where am I?

Where is she?

The cot is empty.

But still he asks, "Was it very painful?"

"Unh hn. Perhaps for you," she replies.

Fulfilled, he moves away from her.

translated by
Maurice Shukla

THE NOWHERE MAN

by J P Das

Bibhu finished his tea and flung the earthen cup on to the rail tracks. He picked up his bag with one hand, held a pile of books in the other and stepped into the corridor, when the train suddenly lurched. Bibhu was quite used to this peculiar behaviour of trains. With steady steps he crossed the corridor and entered the compartment. It was unusually empty.

People say that trains are always crowded, whatever the time or their destination. But Bibhu often came across many unoccupied seats. At such times other hawkers found that their sales slackened, but Bibhu's books sold well. He could talk to the passengers and they were able to glance through the books he offered them.

Casting a quick look over the coach, Bibhu noticed a Bengali couple sitting at one end. He went and sat down opposite them. From his bag he pulled out a thick book in Bangla, and held it out to the man, saying, "You may not know much about the author of this book, but it is going to become famous one day." The gentleman leafed through it and passed it on to his wife. From their faces, Bibhu could tell what kind of book they would buy. So he showed them the latest publication of a popular writer. As expected, the gentleman bought it. After taking the money from him, Bibhu wondered whether to sit down and chat with them or proceed to the next coach. The lady was good-looking. Her sari was expensive and she was wearing some jewellery. But there was no refinement about her. He stood up to go.

Bibhu's friends often asked him, Don't you get bored, wandering up and down on trains like this every day? How would they know that a train is a whole world in itself? People who spend their lives in offices, market-places, homes, amongst neighbours, would never understand that one can build a life for oneself with perfect strangers.

Each morning was, for Bibhu, a fresh wonder. Yesterday's train is not the same the next day. Not only is it in different surroundings, it also takes on a new face. The people in it too are not quite what they were the previous night. But Bibhu did not tell his friends all this. With a laugh he would reply, "You live in a town. My train is my town." After all, what is it that happens outside a train and does not happen in it? In the last ten years of a nomadic existence – why call it a nomadic existence when the train has been his home – how could Bibhu describe all that he had seen? From courtship and love, to estrangement and reconciliation, business, trade, theft, rape, murder, Bibhu had the fortune, or misfortune, of being witness to it all.

Look at what happened the other day. His body went cold just thinking of it. The train had left a major junction. Everyone had finished dinner and was getting ready to sleep. Bibhu decided to make one final round. He crossed the vestibule to enter the adjoining chair-car. A middle-aged woman was standing near the door, a glass jar in her hand. She took a piece of chocolate from the jar and held it out to him. Bibhu took it and put it in his mouth. Then, she took out another piece and stretched out her hand as if to give it to someone standing behind him. Bibhu looked back to see who it was. There was nobody there. He turned around. The woman was gone too! Bibhu's hair stood on end. He quickly stepped into the chair-car and scanned the seats. They were all occupied but not one face was familiar. He went into the next compartment. The woman wasn't there either. Bibhu rushed to the railway attendant, a friend of his, and told him what had happened. "An elderly woman in the chair-car?" asked the attendant, opening out his passenger list. "Here – three women over the age of forty." Bibhu noted their seat numbers and went back. The chocolate lady was not one of them. Had he imagined the whole thing, he wondered. But the taste of the chocolate was still in his mouth! "Go to sleep, Bibhu. We'll see about it tomorrow," his friend said to him.

In the last ten years, Bibhu had made friends with many railway employees. They allowed him to travel without a ticket, stored his books for him and when the need arose, even lent him money. In a way, these people were Bibhu's family. Sometimes one of them, after finishing his duty, would urge Bibhu to get off the train and spend the night with him at the station. Occasionally, Bibhu would agree. If the shops were still open, he would buy a bottle of liquor and take it to his friend's house. Then, sitting in the small room of a railway colony, they would chat late into the night. For Bibhu, these moments were an extension of his life on the train. The house, usually next to the railway track, would vibrate as trains thundered past all night and Bibhu would feel as if he was sleeping on the train.

A break in Bibhu's routine was the occasional visit to his sister, the only family he had. She lived in a village far away and Bibhu always complained about her not having built her house near a railway station. His nephews were fond of him and affectionately addressed him as the wanderer uncle, Bula mamu.

For the time that Bibhu spent with them, he became a part of the family. He helped with the house-work and mixed happily with everyone in the village. But in a week or so, he would get restless. He would fall silent and not play with the children anymore. Everyone knew it was time for him to leave. His nephews would tease, "The travel-bug has bitten our Bula mamu!"

Once he went away, no one knew where he was. He left no address, wrote no letters. In spite of repeated requests he failed to keep in touch. Soon they stopped worrying about him. They were sure that one fine morning he would turn up and stay for a few days.

While he was there Bibhu helped the children with their studies. On one of his visits, his sister said to him, "Stay on a little longer this time. Go when Dipu's exams are over."

Bibhu became wary. This was a ploy to keep him from leaving, he thought. "I came for a day and I've stayed for seven. I have a lot of work to do," Bibhu said to her.

"What work can you have?" his brother-in-law retorted.

"You won't understand, brother, how difficult my work is! I have to go from bookshop to bookshop and settle my accounts with them. If I don't pay them their dues, how will I get books from them next time? Besides, I have left all my belongings with the guards or conductors of different trains. I must keep track of them," Bibhu tried to explain.

"Who asked you to wander around like this?" said his sister indignantly. "Think of this as your own home and stay here. Or, with the money you have left with us, we will build a little room for you nearby. If you feel uncomfortable about staying here without doing any work, you can help your brother-in-law in the fields. He needs some help."

Bibhu laughed the whole idea away. "Do you expect me to take up something new at this age? I'm quite happy just selling my books."

Annoyed by his attitude, she taunted , "Why don't you admit that you enjoy sleeping in trains and eating from platform vendors?"

In all seriousness, Bibhu replied, "That's true. If the bed doesn't sway, how can a man fall asleep? And how tasty food really is at station platforms, I can't tell you! All right, I'll bring you some next time."

And so Bibhu shrugged off all her suggestions. His brother-in law sometimes joked, "Perhaps if a mami were to come along, our Bula mama would settle down!"

No one had been able to persuade Bibhu to marry. Once the matter had gone as far as choosing a bride for him. A girl from their village, widowed soon after her marriage, had come back to live in her own house. People praised her looks and her temperament. Bibhu's sister and brother-in-law insisted that Bibhu should at least see her and dragged him to her house, against his will.

True, the girl was beautiful and good-natured. She talked simply and frankly about her life in her in-laws' house after her husband's death. Bibhu liked the girl. When they returned home, his brother-in-law advised him, "Just close your eyes and say yes, Bibhu. We have known her ever since she was a child. Such a girl comes one's way only by great good fortune."

Bibhu almost agreed. But then he remembered the girl's calm and innocent face. How could he yoke this nice young girl to his nomadic existence? How could he leave her in the house and go away after they were married? If he didn't, what would happen to that other world of his which ran whistling on rails? These were but excuses. In truth, Bibhu was afraid of being tied down. He couldn't imagine himself confined within the four walls of a house. With such a girl he would feel completely bound. He did not give any answer then. Later he wrote to say that he had decided against it. No one talked to him about marriage after that.

It was not that Bibhu disliked women. He sometimes went with his friends to spend the night at Calcutta's Shonagacchi. The house they frequented was run by a decent, god-fearing old woman. All her girls were simple-hearted and gentle. The place was not without its share of rowdies and drunkards making trouble. But by midnight, it became deserted and silent. For Bibhu, it was a good place to spend his free time. With a little money he could buy some food and liquor, and then, he could sleep in peace. At daybreak he would head for the train.

A friend of his had taken him there some time ago. The friend was in love with one of the girls, Mina. For Bibhu he had found Arati, Mina's friend. Soon Bibhu got to know Arati quite well. She shared with him all her joys and sorrows. He had even fetched Arati's seven or eight-year old son from the village and taken both of them around the city for a whole day. Bibhu used to see Arati regularly. Once he did not turn up for several days. When he finally did, Arati burst into tears, turned violent and refused to listen to his explanations. Only when Bibhu promised to visit her every alternate day, did she calm down.

Bibhu never passed that way again.

Bibhu's sister often worried about his being alone. She tried to scare him by reminding him, "It's all right now that you are still young and healthy. What will happen if you fall ill? Who will look after you?" It wasn't as if Bibhu had not thought about this. In fact, once when he was ill, he had been lying on the platform for a whole day till a friend of his from the Railways took him home and looked after him.

Bibhu made up his mind that the next time he fell ill he would go away to a place where no one knew him. He would not trouble anyone. During his wanderings on the trains he had often come across passengers who were ill or dying. Nobody knew who they were. Yet they were taken care of. Sometimes dead bodies were found on the train. Once a body lay on the platform, unclaimed, unidentified, for two days.

Since then Bibhu had one desire. To go to sleep on the train one day and then, be taken off it, dead. An unknown man in an unknown station, causing no trouble, no inconvenience to anyone.

But quickly, he pushed such thoughts away. He must manage for as long as he could. He hadn't been doing so badly after all. Two books had already been sold that morning. He entered the next coach and stood beside a gentleman reading a book. It's strange how those who buy books are usually those who already have them. The gentleman put his book down and looked through the ones Bibhu was carrying. He asked for one or two titles, then bought one so as not to disappoint Bibhu. A woman sitting in the next row asked Bibhu if he had any children's books. He looked at them to see how old the little girl with her was. "I'll get you some in fifteen minutes," he said and noting her seat number, moved away.

Four passengers were playing cards in the next coach. Bibhu stopped to watch them. Just then one of the players got up and handing his cards to Bibhu, said, "Hold them for a moment. I'll be back." Bibhu sat down and was soon absorbed in the game. When the man returned, he said to Bibhu, "No, no, don't get up. Finish this game." Once more Bibhu concentrated on the cards.

When the game was over, Bibhu collected the books from the end of the train and went back to the little girl. She was crying. Handing the books to the mother, he tried to cheer the child up. He pointed to things outside the window, he showed her pictures from books, but she would not stop crying. In the end he took out a kerchief from his pocket, rolled it into the shape of a mouse and made it jump on his arm. Immediately the tears stopped. She smiled from behind her mother's back. Her mother chose a book and gave it to her. She threw it down. Bibhu picked it up and held it out. She would not touch it. Giving Bibhu the money for the book, the lady said, "Leave her alone. Don't spoil her. One slap and she'll be all right." Bibhu walked away.

Later that evening, Bibhu got off at a station to have some tea.

He saw the mother and daughter alight from the train. The girl was smiling. Spotting Bibhu, the mother turned to her daughter and said, "Look! There's the babu who sold us the books. He made you laugh when you were crying. Say namaskar to him." The little girl folded her hands shyly. Bibhu put the cup down and thought he would accompany them till the exit gate. But somehow his feet did not move. What was the point of prolonging the acquaintance?

Countless such friendships had come his way. But he had not allowed any of them to grow. One person he met had offered him a job, another was willing to give him an agency for his company. Once a gentleman approached Bibhu with a letter of introduction from his brother-in-law. It was a proposal. If Bibhu agreed to marry the man's widowed sister, he would inherit all her property. Many such proposals had come to him, but Bibhu had simply laughed them off. What would he do with land and property?

How many people Bibhu met on trains. But he would not remember their faces if he saw them after a week. Once they got off, he forgot them. Sometimes a passenger would tell him, "I met you five years ago on this train. You sold a book at half the price, remember?" Yet another would say, "I have been seeing you for so many years but you have not changed. What secret medicine do you have that keeps you looking the same? You should sell that instead!"

One day Bibhu was walking about at a station when he noticed the same woman and her daughter board the train. This time there was a young lady with them. After a while, the woman got off the train and started talking to the lady inside. Bibhu could not decide whether to go and speak to them or not, when the little girl saw him and smiled. Now Bibhu had to meet them.

Seeing him, the woman said, "We're really lucky to have met you again. My sister is going by this train. She has never travelled alone, so I'm a little worried. My brother has been informed and he will receive her at the station. But it's nice to know that you're on the same train. Please take care of her during the journey."

Bibhu looked through the window. A girl of about twenty or twenty-two was staring at him. A little later the woman said, "Please come closer to the window. Rumi can't see you properly. Just look at her! Such a big girl and still so shy." When Bibhu came closer, Rumi asked, "Which is your coach?" "The same as yours," Bibhu replied. Once the train started, Bibhu went to Rumi and said, "I'll be back soon."

"How can I stay all alone?" she complained. She moved a little to make place for him. Bibhu sat down. I will go later to fetch my books, he thought. Rumi did not say anything more. She just kept looking out of the window. After about ten minutes Bibhu got up. Immediately, Rumi turned to him saying, "I'm thirsty." How very timely! said Bibhu to himself. "I'll fetch you some water," he told her and went to the conductor's cabin, selected the books to put in his bag and arranged those he wanted to carry in his hand. As he got up, he remembered the water. He put the books down, picked up a glass of water and took it to Rumi.

"So long to get a glass of water!" exclaimed Rumi. She took a sip. "Ugh, this water is horrible! Aren't there any orange drinks on this train? I have money with me, you know."

Bibhu laughed. "Drink this now. You can have your orange at the next station." He was about to go, when Rumi asked, "Where are you going?"

"To sell books. That's my job. Let me go now."

"Show me your books. I'd like to buy one." She took the books out of the bag one by one and looked at them. She picked up one.

"I want this one. How much is it?"

"Thirty-three rupees. I'll give it to you for three rupees less."

"That means thirty rupees! Thirty rupees! Who will buy such a costly book? Why don't you sell film magazines? I would have bought one."

Finally, Bibhu got up. "I must go. If I don't sell any books what will I eat?"

"I'll take you to my brother's house. You can eat there. Taste my sister-in-law's cooking once and you'll remember it all your life. How much money do you make every month?"

"I can't say. One month I may sell many books, another month, very few. When that happens, I have to fast."

"So do one thing. Whenever you earn well put some money in the bank. Then, you can manage with the savings if you don't earn enough. Don't you have that much sense?" she asked impudently.

"Very well. From now on I'll put money in the bank. In which bank should I put it?" Bibhu wanted to know.

"I don't know. You're a grown man. Don't you know anything about banks? If you were staying near our house I would have shown you the bank. Where's your house?"

"My house? This is my house," Bibhu replied.

"This train? How lucky! You can go off wherever you want, whenever you want, you can get down at stations to eat piping-hot baras and piyajis or have an orange!"

Just then the TTE entered the coach. Seeing Bibhu, he said, "The book you gave me last time was dreadful. I'll return it tomorrow." The TTE asked Rumi for her ticket, but she did not hear him. Bibhu nudged her, "Show your ticket." She held out her purse to him, "It's inside." Bibhu fished out the ticket from a jumble of notes and coins, keys, kerchief and bits of paper. After he showed the ticket he put it back in the purse, and was about to return it to her, when she said, "Keep it with you. I'll certainly lose it if it remains with me."

The train was entering a station. Bibhu noticed that Rumi looked somewhat grim. When he asked her what was wrong, she just turned away. Bibhu kept quiet thinking her mood would pass. Soon, as he had anticipated, Rumi nudged him hard.

"You promised to get me an orange at this station!"

Bibhu stood up, laughing.

"I gave you the purse to keep it safe. Not to leave it like this on the seat. What if someone steals it?" Rumi scolded.

For the rest of the journey Rumi did not let Bibhu get up. She kept talking to him. Not only was he forced to recount his own life story in minute detail but he had to listen to a host of small, insignificant incidents from her life as well. Bibhu now knew who her chief enemies were, who the worst lecturer in her college was, the kind of man she wanted to marry, the name of her favourite actor, and so on.

At last they arrived at Rumi's destination. Rumi kept insisting that Bibhu should have dinner at her brother's house. They stepped onto the platform. It was getting dark. Rumi looked around but could not see her brother anywhere. Why was he late? Had he not expected the train to be on time? Bibhu told her to sit on a bench, put her luggage beside her and placed the purse in her hands. Saying he was going to look for her brother, he climbed the overbridge and stood at a place from where he could see her. Rumi was sitting on the bench, calmly leafing through the cinema magazine he had bought her.

No, Bibhu thought. There was no question of his going to Rumi's brother's house tonight. But what if the brother did not turn up? He was caught in a most awkward situation.

Just then a man came up to Rumi. Bibhu was saved! But Rumi did not get up. After saying something to her, the man glanced around as if looking for someone.

Furtively, Bibhu walked down the overbridge. Instead of going towards Rumi he moved to the other side of the platform. A passenger train was about to leave in the opposite direction. Bibhu looked back and saw Rumi still there. He peeped into the window of the coach near him and saw a little boy sitting there, a game of Ludo on his lap. He was pestering his father to play with him. But the father was engrossed in a conversation and ignored him.

The whistle blew. The train started moving. From the corner of his eye Bibhu saw that Rumi's brother had returned and Rumi was standing up.

Bibhu jumped into the moving train. He went straight to the little boy and said, "Come, I'll play with you."

translated by
Jasjit Man Singh &
Devinder Kaur
Assa Singh

YUDHISHTER

by Ajeet Cour

T he flood came again. Water, the colour of molasses, rushed through the whole village. Small trees, weak and defenceless, fell to the surging waters, like one hit by a bullet. Thadam! A few large trees survived. The water tore at their trunks, trying to uproot them, but they stood firm like brave and strong warriors.

A storm had raged that night. Thunder rumbled ominously, lightning rent the sky and the rain came down in torrents. The very walls of the mud-built houses shivered as the cold seeped in. Slowly they began to crumble.

The crops, standing waist-high in the fields, were washed away. In the houses, the bhadolian, full of grain, and the mud chulas dissolved in the swirling water. Every article in the houses, from the handwoven khes to the quilts and durries, the charpais and utensils to the wooden plough and yoke, even the animals, everything was carried away by the flood water. The village folk were huddled together on the few roof tops remaining or they clung to the branches of the strong trees.

No dogs barked, no crows cawed. There was silence all around. Silence and fear. And the swirling, rampaging water.

The silence was broken only by the wailing of the children. Cries of hunger and fear. Water everywhere, but not one drop to drink. During a heavy shower, the people would turn their terrified faces to the sky and open their mouths. The drops of rain that they managed to catch soothed their parched mouths, the fire in their throats. For a moment.

Their lives, their very means of existence, had been destroyed by water, yet it was for a sip of water that they now longed. Occasionally someone would be driven to reach down, cup the flood water and drink it. But the sight of a floating corpse, or the bloated carcass of a cow would repel him. He would, instead, simply gulp dry air.

On the fifth day the flood water receded. It left behind slush and mud.

The people descended from their places of refuge. Hunger, which had been subdued by fear for four days, now flared up, demanding to be satisfied. But there was nothing to eat. Nothing. Not one grain.

Only the tall Haveli stood intact. The flood water had battered its solid foundations and walls in vain. The damp had crept into the walls, but everything had been moved to the safety of the upper storeys. The bhadolian were full of grain and the vaddi bebe thought to herself, When it is bright and sunny we will spread the grain on the roof to dry. Then it won't be infested with insects. However, the immediate need was to hide it.

The Haveli was surrounded by countless empty stomachs, driven mad by the pangs of hunger. The residents of the Haveli barricaded themselves against the hordes, fastening the high iron doors. But they could not keep those anguished voices out. The crying of the children, the wailing of the women. The wind carried the sounds up to the parapet and into the Haveli. It left them there, hovering, like ill-omened black-winged birds, waiting to swoop down.

Through the ankle-deep slush, the people, some bent with age, walked with slow, laboured steps towards their devastated homes. Some houses had collapsed completely. Only the walls of others were still standing but the roofs had caved in. Those that had not, steadily dripped their load of water.

They dragged out the soggy twisted charpais which the flood had not been able to carry away – because a leg or a corner got jammed in a doorway – and set them up in the mud covered chaupal. There they sat and discussed what to do next. The young men wanted to appeal to the people of the Haveli. Someone behind the high doors might listen to them. Perhaps a tiny corner of someone's stone heart might melt with pity and loan them half a bhadoli of grain. The elders knew that this course of action was futile. They had been neighbours of these callous folk all their lives! The Haveli people did not even mourn their dead. Their uncaring attitude was typical of their culture. For them, a man's worth lay only in a well stocked house, or a well-fed stomach. People whose stomachs were empty or whose homes had crumbling walls and leaking roofs were vulgar and foolish. But the elders were hungry too. What could they do? To whom could they turn?

Having rained down destruction, the sky finally cleared. It was washed clean, blue and soft, as if nothing had happened. How could the sky look so innocent after the terrible havoc it had wrought?

For a long time they sat on the misshapen charpais, quiet and thoughtful. Perhaps they were not even thinking. With blank, vacuous eyes they stared at their hands lying in their laps like wounded birds. Or they looked helplessly at each other's faces, earthbrown and wet, like the crumbling walls. The children were quiet, exhausted with crying. Occasionally a mother would shudder deeply and sob dry-eyed. The village folk considered it extremely inauspicious, as bad an omen as the howling of dogs at midnight.

Dusk fell. Stars twinkled, as if they were writing the story of a disaster on the clean page of the sky.

Each one thought a thousand thoughts. Thoughts which had no beginning, no end, no substance.

In the dark depths of despair, words become mute and meaningless like scraps of paper scattered by the wind. And silence speaks, resounding with their pain. It fills the vast expanse only to echo back and surround them. They feel a procession of their silent griefs shuffle through the slushy lanes, cling to the walls of their broken homes and wail soundlessly.

The flood tide had turned. But had it really retreated? Or merely paused to see what they would do next? The flood was not just water greedily grasping all it could reach. It was a menacing force, like a bloodthirsty animal lurking in the bushes, stalking its prey, ready to pounce and unleash the power in its bloody claws and khanjar-like fangs.

The ninety-year old Elder, the spokesman of the village, had always called for attention by tapping the ground with his stick and clearing his throat. Today the stick made no sound as it struck the oozing mud. He did not have the strength to cough commandingly either. Nor was it necessary in that shroud of silence.

In a feeble, tremulous voice he asked, "What should we do now?"

All eyes turned to him, bereft of desire, of expectation. When eyes are devoid of these, the birds of Death lay their eggs in them.

He continued in a dead voice, "Shall we ask for help at the Haveli?"

As they got up, the charpais resumed their twisted shapes, and stood with one end off the ground, pointing to the sky.

Wading through the mud they reached the high, iron doors of the Haveli. With weak, tired hands they thumped on the metal door. There was silence. They beat harder, this time with clenched fists. Again silence. Then a young boy grabbed the Elder's stick, gave him his arm to lean on instead, and started banging on the door with the stick.

"Don't, son. If my stick breaks, how will I walk?" pleaded the old man. But the youngster continued to hammer on the door.

From the parapet the sahukar, who was also a moneylender, looked down and shouted, "What do you think you are doing? Is this any time to come? Attacking our house in the middle of the night!"

"We are not attacking, sarkar," the old man mumbled. "We've merely come to plead with you."

"Is this the way to do it? By breaking down the door? You have ruined everyone's sleep, haraamzade!"

The old man's frail body trembled uncontrollably. His grizzled beard, the hair on his chest, yellowed with age, shook, and his voice, born in the last century, quivered as he spoke again, "Not an attack, sarkar. We are dying of hunger ..."

"Hunger?" thundered the sahukar of the Haveli. "Do you think there is a langar opened here for you? Our land is ruined, our crops are washed away, and on top of that you ... in the middle of the night."

It was true. Half the cultivable land in the village belonged to them. The crops had been washed away.

But it was also true that the bhadolian were full of the grain from the last harvest. It was a crop sown, nurtured, harvested, threshed and stored in the Haveli by these peasants. Even those with small holdings worked for the sahukar at harvest time. All for some fodder for their cattle and a few measures of grain for themselves.

"Sarkar, if you could loan us some grain ..."

"Loan? Does anyone loan grain at a time like this? Get out. Go away."

"Where can we go, huzoor? We have nothing. No chulhas, no kulas, no crops, no grain. We have nothing to eat."

By this time the younger son of the zamindar appeared by his father's side, a gun in hand.

"Are you going or shall I fire," he threatened, pointing the muzzle at the crowd.

Frightened, the older people started backing away. But the

youths stood firm, declaring, "Don't move. We are not going anywhere. Stay right here. This is only one door! To satisfy our hunger we can break ten such doors."

"They have a gun," cautioned the elders.

"How many will they kill with one gun? They will run out of bullets. But before that we'll break the door. If we all push together it will fall away like a piece of old paper."

"No, son. We are already half dead."

"Then why be afraid of Death?"

For a few minutes they stood there, arguing. Then the Elder turned and started to walk away leaning heavily on his stick. Perhaps he did not have the courage to see the blood of his children and their children spill before his eyes. No one dared to disregard the Elder. They followed him silently back to their charpais. Pushing them down to the ground, they sat wondering what to do.

The Elder, shading his eyes with his hand, looked up at the sky. Through the bushy white eyebrows, he saw a misted moon. To him it was an open wound on the chest of the heavens, and the stars throbbed with its pain.

"I think we should cross the river. We will look for a living in the big town there. And save our children from starvation. So?" he asked, and waited for consent.

"I say we should break the walls of the Haveli. There is plenty of space and food for all of us," spoke one youth forcefully.

"That is one way. But many will lose their lives. Seeing all those bodies, will we who survive be able to eat? It is better that we cross the river, work hard and feed ourselves. Then, when we are strong, we will find a way to deal with the heartless people in the Haveli. We must teach them a lesson, but the time is not ripe yet," the Elder decreed resolutely despite his quivering voice.

In the middle of the night, they got up from their charpais and quietly made their way to the river. Their animals – buffaloes, cows, calves, and dogs, starved and barely alive, followed them.

The skewed legs of the charpais lifted off the ground once again, as if to watch the exodus. The procession reached the riverside. The river had overflowed its mud banks and left a layer of slush before retreating into its own channel.

In the dim light, the river was pitch black. It flowed sluggishly, having gorged on the carcasses of cattle, stoves, utensils, mud from the walls, tiles from the roofs, quilts and mattresses, thick cotton sheets, clothes, children's sandals, shoes, and even school bags and books. It was sightless, deaf, full of blackness, this water, the other side of which had become one with the darkness. Yet they believed that on the other side was land, much better than the slush on this side.

There was nobody in sight – no boat, nothing. Only the darkness and a faint sibilance. Was it the river? Or the humming in their own ears?

They would wait. They had plenty of patience. And plenty of fortitude. To wait for the morning. For a boat. For a better life. And a new destiny.

Many calamities befall man. He undergoes and endures infinite suffering. But Nature and Time are indifferent to his fate. The earth continues to rotate without pause. Night follows day. The blue sky, the wafting grey clouds, morning and evening, all follow their eternal, immutable laws, unconcerned, while man suffers. He has resilience. But is there any measure of his suffering before the final release?

Gradually the darkness began to fade, the stars to melt. But there were no familiar early morning sounds. No birds twittered, no cocks crowed. No butter was churned. The birds had deserted this desolate land, the pots and churners had been taken away by the flood.

And yet the day did dawn. The disc of the sun floated above the horizon.

The children, comatose with hunger could cry no more. The

elders had experienced hunger so often that their powers of endurance were boundless, like God. But thirst is cruel. Yet they could not dip their cupped hands into the river and wet their parched lips. The sight of the floating carcasses ...

The cows and buffaloes lay in the mud, their heads drooping, eyes glazed, as if they were dreaming. The dogs too were listless, sighing deeply every now and then.

As the sun climbed higher, their bodies became leaden. Their tongues became like blocks of wood and their throats sprouted thorns.

They waited. For a boat to ferry them across the river. To the far bank where the land was different. And the road led to the city where the tall houses were out of reach of the flood. There were bright lights, jobs. There was water to drink. And food. Food ... food ... food.

When one is waiting, a day feels like a century. Time seems to shut its eyes, like cattle, and withdraw into a dream state, coming alive only when sated, like cattle chewing the cud. But a body racked by hunger for five or six day sits still, doubled up, chin sinking on knees, eyes closed. The mind hovers between sleep and half sleep, somewhere between the earth and the heavens, dreaming troubled dreams.

At last the sun set. It had to, but it took forever. Night fell. A deep, dark night. The moon played hide and seek for a while, then disappeared. Only the shards of stars remained. The ground, the river, the sky, all dissolved into a uniform blackness.

Centuries passed. Perhaps ages. Perhaps aeons.

Suddenly, in the distance, they glimpsed a dim, flickering light. The elders, shading their eyes with their hands, fixed their gaze on it. Everyone stood up – young men, boys and girls, women and children – to gaze at the flickering light.

"Perhaps it is a boat," the oldest of them all said in an unsteady voice.

"Yes."

"The lantern must be hanging from the mast ..."

At times the light seemed to be coming closer. At others it seemed to be moving away. Some began to wonder if they were only imagining it.

Slowly the light approached them. They could see the swaying lantern clearly now and hear the splash of the oars. Yes. It was a boat. A boat with a man in it.

The boat drifted to the shore. Everyone surrounded the mallah and begged him to take them across.

He was very tired. "I am going to sleep," he told them.

"Sleep? Is this any time to sleep? Whole villages have been washed away, the land is a swamp ... Where will you sleep? Look at us. We have not slept for days. First we were clinging to the roofs, hanging from the branches, hungry and thirsty. Now we have been sitting here, waiting ..."

"I lost my way and came this side. I usually find my way by the stars but in this pitch darkness ... I don't know what happened. The river has become so wide. Once you leave the bank you don't know where the current will take you."

"Never mind. We will all rest once we reach the other side. There we will eat and sleep. But just take us across."

"Are there any langars open there? It is the same everywhere. Darkness and starvation. You stay here and let me also rest."

The Elder pleaded again, in desperation.

"We will all die! Not one of us will survive, waiting for the morning ... Even if we don't get food, at least we will have water to drink." Then changing his tone, he invoked blessings on the boatman, "May your children live long. May you thrive ... Just take us across."

The mallah softened. In a resigned voice he said, "Come. Get into the boat. Be careful. But leave your cattle here. The God who created them will also put food in their mouths."

Everybody knew that was not true. But what could they do? The boat wasn't a Noah's Ark that cows and buffaloes, camels and horses, bullocks and hares, lions and jackals, dogs and squirrels, crows and sparrows, parrots and human beings could all be carried across the river. They crowded into the boat. Some sat, others stood holding on to the mast.

One handsome young boy tried to get into the boat with a black-and-white dog in his arms. He was called Mangtoo. His mother had given him this name to ward off the evil eye. She had prayed to Pirs and Fakirs, lighted lamps at shrines and made offerings at graves of holy men, for the gift of a son.

The mallah scolded him. "The boat is already overloaded. There's hardly any room for human beings, you want to bring your dog!"

Mangtoo was distressed. "But this is Moti," he cried.

"I don't care if it is a moti or a heera. My boat is not for dogs. Come if you want, but leave the dog behind."

Mangtoo stepped back at once. In a firm and steady voice, he declared, "If Moti can't go, I won't go either."

Mangtoo's mother had died a long time ago. Mangtoo's father had taken a loan from the sahukar. To repay that loan, Mangtoo worked for the sahukar in the Haveli and looked after the cattle. For this he was given food which he shared with Moti. Whenever he was lonely or upset, Mangtoo would open his heart out to his companion.

Everyone knew of this deep affection between the boy and his dog. That is why no one could say to him, Why do you want to put your life in danger? Come. Get into the boat. We will all return one day, when things are better. Your Moti will wait for you. The same God who created him will ...

No one said a word. Only the Elder called out to him once. But his voice was drowned in the sound of the waves.

The boat moved away.

The buffaloes, cows and calves, were all left behind. In the dark no one could see their eyes. Perhaps they were weeping. Or perhaps they had simply shut their eyes.

When all hope is lost, one experiences a kind of tranquillity, a release. Perhaps that is what Mahatma Buddha experienced when he sat under the Bodhi tree.

Mangtoo stood there with Moti in his arms, and watched the light of the swaying lantern slowly dissolve in the distance.

The people in the boat were overcome by a strange feeling, as if they were between reality and unreality. At times they felt they were actually in the boat as it hiccuped along on the swollen water. At others, they felt they were still sitting on the bank, surrounded by their cattle and the mangy dogs of the village, watching the wide river flow. And it was the mud-covered earth below them that was shaking.

Time seemed to stand still.

While they waited for the boat, the hope of reaching the other side was like a flame in their hearts. But now, when they were actually in the boat, moving towards it, that hope itself seemed to be dying, the flame turning to ashes. Just as fish float to the top of the water tank when they are dying, and turn their white bellies to the sky when dead, they too began to lose the desire to reach the other side.

The mallah was really very tired. For a while, they could hear the splashing of his oars. Soon, he just let them trail in the current.

Nobody knew how far they had travelled or how much farther it was to the other shore. All around them was deep darkness. Not a star was seen.

A long time passed. Hours, weeks, months, years, centuries, aeons. That is what they felt. But it was the same night.

Suddenly, the boatman slumped in his seat. He let go of both oars. Perhaps deliberately or perhaps they slipped out of his tired, wooden hands. The oars were swept away with a soft sound. Like a sound in a disturbed dream. A disembodied sound which is in reality no sound at all.

Seeing this, those near him groped for the oars. But there were no oars! Word of this new calamity spread through the boat. Encircled by the opaque darkness, far away from land, in the middle of the death-gorged river, they found themselves besieged. Terrified screams rose from their throats only to be swallowed by the water.

Then one man got up. The wrestler. With exercise and oil massage he used to keep himself fit and strong. He would rub mud on himself, and wrestle at the village fair, making his destiny. The days of his youth were long past now, but he was still full of courage, and determination. He stripped off his shirt, folded his tehmat and tied it around his hips like a loin cloth. Then he spoke.

"Don't worry. I will swim to the other bank. There I'll arrange for oars, or find another boat. You stay here. Don't move about or the boat will capsize. I'll be back very soon."

"It's no use," said the Elder in a voice that already seemed dead. "It is not easy to swim the swollen river."

"One doesn't always do what is easy, Bapuji," he replied, in a respectful yet firm voice. And he dived into the river with a splash.

His dive was as sure as his voice. And the splash was the thunk of any brave and strong body as it struck water. For some time they could hear his arms slice through the water. Then the sound became fainter and fainter.

The river was very wide. Courage alone was not enough to cross it. Gradually his arms and legs became wooden and stiff. He felt as if a stone was tied to his waist. The force of the water was much greater than his hard-earned stamina. It was dragging him under. His nose and mouth filled with the foetid, corpse-soaked water and he didn't have the strength to surface and spit it out.

As he drowned, a scream – intensified by all the strength of the past years – tore out of him. It rose to the sky like a whirlwind as if it would pierce the very heart of the heavens. It spread over the black water like the hissing of many thousand Shesh nags. It rippled through the entire universe. In the distant towns, the lights went out with a bang, like burnt-out crackers. And once more darkness lay over the land and over the sky.

But the drowning man did not drown. He left behind his scream. And in the anguish of that brave man's scream was contained all the cruelty, all the cowardice and all the potential that man is capable of.

In the boat, Fear cringed in the face of a capricious destiny and Death proudly staked its claim.

On the bank which had been forsaken, Mangtoo stood for a long time, watching the boat as it disappeared into the blackness. He wondered where it might have reached.

Then, hugging Moti, his companion, his friend, his confidant, close to his chest, he turned and walked away.

Turned his back on the darkness. Into the darkness. Alone. Determined.

As he walked, he rested his cheek against Moti's. It felt wet.

"Why are you crying, yaar? You are not alone. Nor am I. Together we will reach somewhere."

Moti growled softly in his throat. As if he agreed. But the tears continued to flow.

Mangtoo recalled an incident from a long time ago. The old woman in the house near the banyan tree had once said to him, "If we love dogs, their hearts too fill with love. They cannot speak, but they can cry!"

Mangtoo tucked Moti's face under his chin and walked on. With no direction, no hope, no life, no death. Perhaps not even Heaven or Hell.

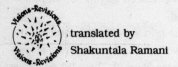

translated by
Shakuntala Ramani

THE HAPPENING

by Na Muthuswamy

They say I was three years old when I first fell into a well. Thirty years have passed since, and I have acquired much experience of falling into wells of all kinds. There is a difference between falling into a domestic well and one used for irrigation.

A domestic well is less dangerous. It has walls with built up sides and a rope is suspended from a pulley. The coir pulley-rope comes sliding down over the pulley and does not hamper your fall. Also, in such wells there is ample room all around you.

In an irrigation well, there are no walls. The circumference is bisected by a beam placed over shaky stones. A shaft sticks out from the cross beam. This central shaft is stiff and inflexible unlike the rope. Sometimes a water scoop is suspended from it. This restricts the space within the well even further.

When I was three, I fell into a well of the pulley-rope kind. Just as one gets used to animals, one can get used to ropes, I suppose! The rope did not bruise me, I am told.

When my father built this house he had a wall made around the well. Until then it had been an old well without walls. Who knows how many generations had drawn water from it! They did not have a pulley, so they must have put a log across the mouth and drawn water with a pot tied to a stout rope. Apparently, they had done this from all sides, for the inner circumference had become blunted by frequent banging of the brass pots. The whole well seemed to be made of a single, circular piece of stone. Such was the well as I remember it.

Some bricks had fallen out of the inner wall, leaving gaping holes. For most of the year, these holes were above the water level and sparrows built their nests in them. Whenever a bucket was let into the well the sparrows would flutter about in panic, dashing against each other.

Once during a violent storm, a tamarind tree was uprooted. It lay upside down, between the well and the hay-stack, with its roots growing into the sky as it were. When this tree was blasted with gunpowder to break it up for a brick kiln, a couple of bricks were dislodged. They fell into the well carrying a nest with them. The birds flew away but their offspring, just hatched, wingless, with beaks wide open for food, fell into the water and died. The nest floated on the water. So did some soft, downy feathers.

Plants grew in the crevices, nourished by the droppings of crows. Whenever they were removed, a few bricks fell out. At some places towards the top, the bricks were crumbling and white with age. Below them and just above the water level, there were cobwebs liberally covered with red brick dust. Abandoned by the spiders, they now hung like limp red rags here and there. There were no steps down which one could go to clear the cobwebs. Nor did anyone attempt to remove them in any other way. The cobwebs were automatically cleared away when they struggled to lift me out of the well.

To us the well was just another deep water tank that was built into the ground. At the height of summer, the water level would go down to about a foot. Towards the evening, after water had been drawn to fill the cattle troughs, the sandy bottom would emerge, like the dry bed of the Kaveri. One foot of water seeped in during the night and that was our supply for the whole day. One summer, we tried to deepen the well by digging below the base ring, thinking that the water holes might be clogged. The bottom of the well became muddy. The wall began to give way on one side. To dig further would have endangered the well. So the attempt was given up. Apart from this one change, the well remains as it was when I fell into it that summer.

It was a hot day in the month of Chittirai, redolent with the smell of sunbaked earth, and not even a dry breeze to stir the trees standing in silent stupor. As daylight deepened into dusk, I fell into the well.

The maid had filled the water troughs in the cattle shed and left. The male servant too had gone after pulling out some hay from the stack and leaving it outside. He was not allowed into the inner courtyard. Hay had to be brought in for the suckling calf, kept in the inner courtyard. It could not be left in the shed with the older cattle for they would butt it with their horns. Besides, it might free itself during the night and drink up its mother's milk. Or the cow may manoeuvre itself into a position where the calf could reach its udder. This particular cow was popularly known as the "rogue" cow.

Paati, my grandmother went outside to fetch the bundle of hay left by the servant near the shed. She could easily have taken some from the pile in the cattle shed, but she was afraid that the fierce racing bull kept there would react violently to her coloured sari. Appa was very proud of his bull. He claimed that nobody else possessed so fearsome a beast as this one. When it was yoked to the cart and stood in front of our house, women in the street were afraid to pass near it. This amused Appa and added to his pride.

It was out of a fear of this beast that Paati went to the backyard to fetch the hay. I ran behind her with a rag in my hand. She saw me just as she was opening the wicket gate to enter the backyard. "Go, go," she said, "go inside. There may be insects about."

I turned towards the house. Paati, satisfied that I would go in, walked on. As soon as she disappeared from sight, I emerged from behind the door and took off towards the well.

The pulley had not yet been taken down and put away in the courtyard. It was likely to be stolen if it remained out all night, so it was brought inside after the hay was put out for the calf. Usually, Paati brought it in after washing the haydust from her hands.

The bucket was on the top of the wall around the well. It was not a circular but a square shaped wall, low and wide and convenient to sit on. The rope lay coiled nearby. Close to the well, a granite slab supported on pieces of tiles, was placed for washing clothes. I wanted to dip my rag in the water and wash it on the stone. I could not reach the bucket nor was I tall enough to climb on to the wall. So I must have got on to the granite slab and from there reached the top of the wall. The bucket was empty. Now, can one wash clothes without water? I must have decided, Let's play with the bucket at least, and got into it.

It was a big bucket, large enough to completely hold a three-year old. I was anxious that Paati should not see me, I suppose, so I must have peeped out to see if she was coming. The concrete pillar, built to support the cross-beam of the pulley, must have obstructed my view. I probably leaned over to look beyond it, holding on to the rim of the bucket. The bucket slipped and fell. I should have been thrown into the water but it did not happen that way. I must have had a firm grip on the bucket for I remained inside it as it fell into the well. The rope came sliding down the pulley until the bucket reached the water. The end of the rope was pulled free and it fell on top of me. Not the entire weight of the rope, since half of it fell into the water.

My memory of the incident is hazy now, dim like the bottom of the well when darkness closes in. They lowered a lantern into the well to see if I was inside it. Half way down, the flame flickered and died out. Then somebody, who had a torch, shone the light inside.

It seems I was sitting in the bucket holding on to the rope. I do not remember if I was crying. I was not hurt. In its swift descent to the bottom, the bucket had dropped straight down without hitting the sides. The rapid fall must have made my young heart jump up into my throat. The heart gives a jolt, even if one steps into a small puddle in the dark. When the raised foot encounters an emptiness beyond the pressure exerted to place it on firm ground, it seems to go limp. The brain registers the shock and the flesh under the skin has a raw bruised feeling. I wonder if one feels all this when one is just three years old.

I experienced such a feeling later when I fell into the irrigation well next door, as I was pushing down the water scoop. While trying to place my foot on the cross beam, I misjudged the distance. There was nothing under my feet. My heart jolted then, as I fell into the well. Things happened in rapid succession as I fell, each new bruise driving out the memory of the previous one. The water scoop slipped from my hands and hit me squarely in the face. The crossbar scratched my ribs. My head banged against a step set inside the well, and pieces of my skin and hair were plastered on to the stone. This time, I had fallen into a well with plenty of water. My body burned when the bruised portions came into contact with the water.

When I had fallen into the well earlier, sitting inside a bucket, I had no bruises. But surely I would have felt the jolt when the bucket landed at the bottom. Perhaps the fall was cushioned by the small amount of water inside the well. Even so, I must have experienced a shock. The darkness inside the narrow confines of the well must surely have frightened me. On top of me lay the wet coir rope. I was surrounded by water even though it was not deep. I must have fainted with the shock. Or I might have remained conscious, shrinking with fear inside the bucket and holding on to it desperately.

It took a long time for them to rescue me. It was quite a while before they realised where I was. Even Paati who had been near the haystack, did not know I had fallen into the well.

Paati had, in fact, been caught by the very bull she was trying to avoid. Either the servant had forgotten to tie it up or else it had broken loose from the shed. As soon as it saw Paati, it charged at her. She could not run back towards the gate so she ran northward. It chased her. Cut off from the gate on the southern end, Paati ran round and round the stack with the bull right behind. Catching hold of a plaited straw rope hanging from the stack, Paati heaved herself to the top. The bull stood below looking at her and waiting. Steadying herself, she moved to the opposite end. The haystack shook, but the bull remained where it was. She cautiously slid down the southern end of the stack. Some of the hay came down with her and fell on top, covering her. The bull came around and gored her with its horns through the hay.

Her terror reached a peak. It also provided her with the impetus to shed it. She had been terrified of being attacked by the bull. That had happened and it would continue to happen. She decided that it might as well happen while she was running. Besides the number of times the bull could get at her would be less if she was moving, and depending on how soon she started off and how fast she ran, she could reduce the attacks ever further. She sprang up and started running with the hay clutched to her body. The bull followed her, butting her with its horns. She crossed the gate and slammed it shut before the bull could pass through. It got stuck in the wattled frame. Paati ran beyond the well. By the time the bull could extricate itself she had reached the house. She closed the door behind her and stood there panting.

"Sell the damn animal, I keep telling him," she gasped, "but will he ever listen to me! Is he waiting for somebody to be killed?" She went to the courtyard and sat down. Amma was lighting a lamp to place in the front room.

"The boy is nowhere to be seen," Amma remarked as she went outside. "Hardly out of the cradle, and he is already roaming the streets. Where on earth could he have gone?" She had not noticed me going out of the back door with Paati.

Annoyed that her distress had not been noticed, Paati taunted, "Growing up to be just like his father." She put her hands up to her head and leaned back to sit more comfortably. She probably assumed that I had been frightened by her warning about the insects, come back into the house, and later gone out through the front door.

After placing the lighted lamp in the front, Amma went up and down the street looking for me. "Can't find him anywhere. He must be sitting in somebody's house." Turning to Paati, she asked, "Did you bring the bucket in?" Paati was seething with anger that Amma had not noticed her plight. Shaken and dazed by her recent experience it did not strike her then that my absence had anything to do with the well.

"How could I have brought it in," she retorted. "That vehicle of Lord Shiva, the Rishabha Vahana which your husband has so lovingly brought home, is standing guard over the bucket like the vehicle of Yama. Who will take it away? No woman will dare go near it. Only a man can attempt it and for that it has to get darker still."

"He is not home either" said Amma, referring to Appa. "Let me see if I can get hold of somebody," she remarked as she went out.

Kannusami, the broker, was walking along the street, eastwards. He was close to my father and assisted him in the buying and selling of cattle. He suffered from hydrocele and could not walk much, so he usually went everywhere with Appa in the bullock cart.

"Kannusami, did you not go with Ayya to Sembanarkoil?" enquired Amma. It was her way of saying, "Come inside. I have work for you."

He understood that. "No. I didn't," he replied, coming up the steps. "Hasn't he returned yet?"

"Really! The kind of animals you purchase and bring home, you and Ayya," she accused. "That bull is out near the well. Go and tie it up" she said, justifying her claim on his services.

He came inside. Paati was sitting in the shadow of the lantern hanging from the rafters. Seeing her he asked, "How is it you are sitting in the dark Periyamma?"

"Get rid of that messenger of Death before stepping into this house again, Kannusami," she said with some heat. "This is the last time I'm telling you."

"Periyamma seems to be very angry," laughed Kannusami from where he stood.

"That animal tried to finish me off today and plaster me all over the haystack. Shouldn't I be angry?" As Kannusami went to the back door, she called out, "Bring back a bundle of hay."

He had hardly crossed the outer courtyard when Amma shouted from the kitchen, "Also get the bucket from the well, Kannusami."

"All right," he said and left.

After tying up the bull, he went out again and fetched hay for the calf. "Amma, there is no bucket on the well," he said. "Only the pulley is there. The bucket must have fallen in."

That was when my absence and the well registered together in Paati's mind. Jumping up from where she sat, she ran out, crying, "Ayyo! the child must have fallen into the well." "Kanna, my child!" screamed Amma, running behind her. Kannusami picked up the lantern and followed them.

By now the news spread down the street. From the street it was carried to the main road as people passed it on, each one claiming to have heard it first.

The servant who had left the house after feeding the cattle, was at the betel shop in the market place. He was standing there, crushing tobacco in his palm, when somebody told him, "Your Ayya's child has fallen into the well." Glad now that he had lingered to buy tobacco, he took off towards Sembanarkoil. So fast did he run that he was able to convey the news to Appa even before I was fished out of the well. And Appa reached the well as I was being brought out. Even now, everyone in that region talks about how swiftly he ran that day.

How fast can a two-legged creature run anyway? He does not have four legs like a horse, does he? Can he run like the wheel which revolves even faster with its many spokes like so many legs? He can, at best, add his two hands to his legs and make it four. Only by turning cartwheels can a man run like a four-spoked wheel.

I can see him running, even today, in my mind's eye. Like the blades of the table fan, his arms and legs vanish in a blur, while his head rotates in the middle like the hub of the fan. On either side of the road, trees rush towards the fields hitting against each other. The groves on the roadside seem as though they are revolving in the opposite direction. Banana plantations swirl and fall in a blur of green. Everything whirls around at great speed, with him at the epicentre. To the left and the right of him they revolve in a semi-circle, falling back as he pushes forward.

It seems he was panting like a dog when he reached and could not speak. He had laboured for our family like a beast of burden. He had remained faithful like a dog. Like a dog his tongue was pink and clean, not scum-coated like a man's. The dog's tongue drips saliva when it pants, but his tongue became dry, proving that he was human after all. It stuck to the roof of his mouth and uncurling it with difficulty, he spoke. "The child has fallen into the well!"

"Where ... Where?" shouted Appa as he came running out from the shop where he had been sitting.

The servant's ribs were heaving. He gasped as he tried to speak. The words stuck in his dry throat, refusing to come out. He tried to swallow his saliva to moisten his throat but could not.

Appa realised that the servant was in no condition to talk. "Get the cart ready, quick," he ordered.

The man untied the bullocks from the pungan tree near the shop and yoked them to the cart. Without waiting for him, Appa leaped on to the cart and took the reins into his own hands. The cart sprang forward on to the Kaveripoompattinam road and raced towards the fields.

These bullocks had been purchased by Kannusami and trained by Appa. They seemed to sense his innermost thoughts, smell his urgency through the bridle which he held in his hands. We have four legs each, they seemed to be saying. Four and four make eight. Add to that the spokes of the wheels. With so many legs we should run faster. We will run faster. And so they did. The mud on the road flew from their speeding hooves and splattered on to the wheel. A well-bred bull never runs with its head lowered. They too ran with their heads held high, froth dripping from their mouths,

Kannusami could not run. Picking up a coil of rope lying in the inner courtyard, he proceeded slowly towards the well. He had already planned how he would get into the well. Since he could not spread his legs and brace them against the wall of the well, he had decided to lower himself down with the help of the rope.

Amma and Paati were standing near the well, wailing loudly. They were not able to see inside the well by the light of the lantern. Kannusami told Amma to fetch a jute rope. He slipped the stout rope he had brought around the pulley and lowered it into the well, taking care that it did not land on me. By then Amma had brought the jute rope. He tied the lantern to it and asked Amma to lower it into the well. He caught hold of the stout rope and started sliding down its length. Along with him, the lantern also came down but when it was half way through the flame flickered and died out. The well was again steeped in darkness. By now a lot of people had gathered around. One of the men had brought a torch and he shone it down the well.

They could see me sitting inside the bucket. Kannusami had also reached the bottom. "The child is alive! The child is alive!" he shouted and gathered me into his arms. His palms were bruised and bleeding because of the rope. Some of the blood dripped on to my body.

The question now was – How were we to be lifted out? If I was hauled up in the bucket, I might fall. Kannusami, too, would not be able to climb up on his own. Both of us had to be taken out together.

They brought a large water scoop, tied ropes to the loops on all four sides and lowered it into the well. Kannusami sat in the centre of the scoop, holding me on his lap. Four people, one on each side of the well, carefully pulled us out.

Appa had come back from Sembanarkoil. It seems he was shaken by the sight of the blood on my body as he took me into his arms.

Then somebody shouted, "That's only Kannusami's blood."

Kannusami stood there, blood trickling down his trembling hands. Appa told him, "Kannusami you saved my son today. Hereafter you shall get a kalam of paddy from me every month for as long as I live."

Everyone in the crowd praised Appa's generosity. Kannusami stood there smiling weakly.

Till the day he died, Kannusami loved to recount the tale of his descent into the well. I remember how I used to run, eager to escape, whenever he started the story.

translated by
Sara Rai

BIJOOKA

by Surendra Prakash

Hori, of Premchand's story, had grown old. So old that his eyebrows and eyelashes were grey, his back was hunched over, and the veins on his hands stood out in a visible pattern on rough, dusky skin.

During this time, two sons had been born to him. But they were no longer alive. One had drowned while bathing in the Ganges. The other was killed in a police encounter. There is not much to tell about the encounter with the police. When one is at peace with one's inner self, but lives in the midst of restlessness, a confrontation with the police becomes inevitable.

Hori's sons had left behind their wives and their children, five in all – two born of the son who had drowned and three of the one killed in the police encounter. The burden of their upkeep now passed to Hori. Blood flowed with renewed vigour through his ageing body.

Old Hori's hands, clutching the

plough, relaxed for a moment. Then his grip tightened once more. He yelled out to his oxen, and the plough moved forward, rending the breast of the earth.

That morning, the sun had not risen yet. A rosy glow spread across the sky. The five children were naked, bathing at the well in Hori's courtyard. The older bahu drew the water and poured it on the children by turns as they splashed around joyfully. The younger bahu was making huge rotis and carefully putting them away in a changri.

Inside the hut, Hori was already dressed and in the process of tying his turban. Having done that, he glanced at himself in the mirror placed in a niche in the wall. A face furrowed with lines looked back at him. Then he turned and stood in front of a picture of Hanumanji, his head bowed, eyes shut and hands folded. Coming out into the yard, he called out, "Is everyone ready?"

"Yes, Bapu!" they replied, in one voice. His bahus straightened the pallu of their saris, their hands beginning to move faster. It was quite obvious to Hori that no one was ready yet. We cannot live without lies, he thought. These lies are so vital for our existence. If God had not given us the gift of lies, we could not live. It all begins with a lie. The effort to pass the lie off as a truth keeps a man alive for years.

Hori's grandchildren and bahus set out to prove the truth of the untruth they had just uttered. Meanwhile, Hori was busy gathering the tools they would need for harvesting. By the time that was done, the others were, indeed, ready.

The rays of the sun cast a magical aura around their house. Their mood was festive. Today they would reap the harvest. Full of enthusiasm, they were impatient to reach the field, their green, golden field, swaying in the breeze.

These were good times indeed, thought Hori, settling the red-and-white checked angochha more comfortably on his shoulder. One did not have to put up·with the bullying of the overseer or be wary of the bania, suffer the tyranny of the angrez or the greed of the zamindar.

Happiness burst like fireworks in their hearts as images of golden crops floated before their eyes.

"Come on, Bapu!" His eldest grandson took his hand, while the others latched on to his legs. The older bahu shut the door of the house. The younger one put the changri of rotis on her head.

Uttering the name of Bir Bajrang Bali, they trooped out into the lane.

The village was already bustling with activity. Groups of people could be seen moving towards their fields. Others were wending their way back to the village.

Life today was somehow different from yesterday. Or so Hori felt.

He turned to glance at the children following him. What else could children of peasants look like? Dark and sickly, they would probably scurry away at the sound of a jeep. Even the changing seasons would alarm them. His bahus, too, were no different from the widows of other peasants. Faces obscured behind pallus, like the wretched lice lurking in the folds of their clothes.

Hori walked on, his head bent. From a distance, he and his family resembled insects of myriad hues, crawling in the dry grass.

Beyond the last house in the lane were the wide, open fields. The water wheel nearby stood still. A dog slept peacefully under a neem tree. Cattle, content after a meal, rested in their enclosures. The fields were a golden expanse in the distance.

Old Hori's land lay beyond these fields, across the canal. It stretched out languorously, waiting for him. Where Hori's field ended, began a vast tract of barren land – parched land, with not a speck of green. Your feet would sink in if you tried to walk on that fallow, crumbling soil. The earth there easily turned to dust, just as the bones of his sons had turned into ash when they were cremated. Ash which scattered like sand at the merest touch.

The wasteland was gradually moving in, towards his field. Hori noticed that in the last fifty years it had advanced by two yards. He did not want it to swallow up his field before his grandchildren grew up. By that time, he too would have become dust. A part of some such barren land.

The path ahead seemed endless, but the bare feet of Hori and his family moved resolutely forward ...

The sun was peering over the eastern horizon. The long walk had made their feet dusty. Farmers, reaping the crop in the neighbouring fields, called out, "Ram-Ram!" and continued with renewed zest, the golden stalks falling under scythes that moved rhythmically.

They crossed the canal, one by one. There was no sign of water, not even enough to create an illusion of it. The water that had once flowed through it had etched strange patterns in the dry sandy soil.

The golden field came into sight and their hearts lit up with joy. Once the crop was cut, their yard would be full of hay, and the hut full of grain. What a pleasure it would be to sit on the charpai, gorging on rice! And how they would belch!

Suddenly Hori froze in his tracks. Those following him stopped too. Hori stared at the field, horrified. The others looked first at Hori, then at the land, trying to fathom what had happened. Something shot through Hori's body like a thunderbolt. He stumbled forward screaming, "Abbe, who is it ...?"

Just then they noticed a strange movement in the middle of the waving field. They followed Hori with quick steps. Hori shouted again, "Abbe, who is that? Who's in my field? Say something, will you? Who is cutting my crop ...?"

There was no reply. They were almost in the field now and could hear the swish of the moving scythe clearly. They stopped, a little unnerved. Tightening his grip on the scythe he held in his hand, Hori challenged, "Haraamzade, speak up."

Slowly, an apparition was seen rising at the far end of the field. A figure that seemed to be smiling at them. And then they heard it speak.

"It's me, Hori Kaka ... me, the bijooka, the scarecrow!" it said, brandishing the sickle it held in its hand.

Stifled screams of fear escaped them. Colour fled their faces. Hori's parched lips turned white. They were stunned into silence. For how long? A moment, a century, an age? Who knows! They were lost to everything around them. The sound of Hori's rasping voice, quivering with rage, jolted them back to the present.

"You ... bijooka ... you! I made you from bits of straw to keep a watch on my crops. I dressed you in the khaki clothes of the angrez shikari whom my father helped. The shikari had left them behind as a token of appreciation. I made your face with a pot, discarded from my house. I placed the angrezi hat on your head. And now, you lifeless puppet, you dare to reap my crop?"

Hori advanced as he spoke. The bijooka, not in the least perturbed by what Hori had just said, grinned at them. As they came closer, they saw that a fourth of the crop had already been harvested. And there the bijooka stood, smiling, sickle in hand. Where could it have got the sickle from, they wondered. Hadn't it been under their watchful eyes all these months, standing there, lifeless, empty-handed? And today ... why, it could have been a man! A flesh and blood person, no different from them!

The sight of it standing there, drove Hori out of his mind. He lunged forward and gave the bijooka a violent shove. It did not budge. But with the impact of the blow, Hori was hurled to the ground. Screaming, the people behind Hori ran up to him. He was struggling to rise, one hand supporting his back. They helped him up. He stared at the bijooka, a frightened look on his face, and said, "So you have become stronger than me, bijooka! I, who made you with my own hands, to stand vigil over *my* crop!"

Smiling as always, the bijooka spoke, "There is no need to be so upset, Hori Kaka. I have only taken my share of the crop ... one-fourth, that's all."

"Why? Who are you? What right do you have to a share at all?"

"I do have a claim to the crop, Hori Kaka. Because I am. I exist. And because I have kept watch over this field."

"I put you there, knowing you had no life. How can a lifeless object have rights? Besides where did you get that?" Hori asked, pointing to the sickle.

The bijooka guffawed loudly. "Hori Kaka ... you are talking to me and yet you insist I am lifeless!"

"But how did you get the sickle? And life? You had neither when I made you."

"Well, it happened on its own ... The day you split the bamboo to make my frame, dressed me in the angrez shikari's rags, etched eyes, nose, ears and mouth on a broken pot - even that day, life was seething in all these things. When they were put together, I came into being. Meanwhile the crop was ripening, and I stood there, biding my time. A sickle slowly began to take form within me. By the time the harvest was ready, so was the sickle. The sickle you see in my hands. However, I did not betray the trust you had placed in me. I waited patiently for this day. Now when you are ready to reap the harvest, I too have taken what is due to me. What is wrong with that?"

The bijooka spoke in a slow, deliberate manner. The import of its words was immediately clear to all of them.

"But this is impossible ... it's a conspiracy against me. As far as

I'm concerned, you are not alive. Don't think you can get away with this, you schemer! I'll go to the panchayat. Put that sickle down. I won't let you take a single stalk," Hori yelled.

The bijooka flung the sickle away, the smile still fixed on its face.

The panchayat met in the chaupal. It was to take a decision that day. Both the concerned parties had already stated their claims. The sarpanch and the panch were present. Hori sat in their midst with his grandchildren. Signs of deep anguish were imprinted upon his pale face. His bahus stood with the other women. They were all waiting for the bijooka.

At last, they spotted the bijooka in the distance, ambling along. Smiling, of course. All eyes were lifted towards it. There was something about its appearance that commanded respect. As it entered the square, everyone stood up. Involuntarily, they bowed their heads. The sight disturbed Hori. He couldn't ignore the niggling feeling that the villagers had allowed their conscience to be bought by the bijooka. So had the panchayat, it seemed. He felt helpless, desperate – like a drowning man wildly thrashing his limbs.

The sarpanch announced the verdict. A tremor went through Hori as he agreed to give the bijooka a fourth of his crop. Then he rose to his feet and addressed his grandsons.

"Listen. This is probably the last harvest I will live to reap. The arid land hasn't reached our field yet. My advice to you is this, Never set up a bijooka to guard your crop. When the field is ploughed next year and the seeds are sown, and the nectar of rain brings forth new shoots, bind me to a pole and stand me up in the field instead of a bijooka. I will look after your crops till your fields are swallowed by the arid waste and the soil turns to dust. Don't ever remove me. Let me stand testimony to the fact that you did not make a bijooka. A bijooka is not lifeless as it is supposed to be. Indeed, it acquires a life of its own. And this fact of existence itself invests it with a sickle. To say nothing, of course, of its right to a fourth of the harvest."

Having said this, Hori trudged towards his field. His grandchildren walked behind him, followed by the two bahus. Then came the villagers, with slow unhurried steps, their heads drooping low.

They had almost made it to the field when Hori collapsed. His grandchildren immediately set themselves to the task of tying him to a pole, under the curious eyes of the spectators. The bijooka took off the shikari's hat, held it against its chest and bowed its head.

A FINAL WORD

Today, we accept that translation is a complex political act and the ethics hard to define. The translator has to choose individual strategies to negotiate between the demands of two different languages, cultures, class and and often gender. For us at Katha, each translation effort entails a reconsideration of some recurrent issues – What are the touchstones for judging a translation? If the act of translation is really a process, when should the focus shift from the conventions of the source language to those of the target language? Are group translation efforts likely to be more successful than individual attempts? And, how creative should the translator be? Or how self-effacing?

Katha organised a workshop for the winners and runners-up of the translation contest to provide a forum to discuss its concerns regarding translations. Distinguished literary personages like Gita Hariharan, C.T. Indra, Lakshmi Kannan, Ranga Rao, Harish Trivedi, Nirmal Verma and Rajendra Yadav participated in the discussion, articulating some fresh issues and putting to rest a few of the old ones.

The focus of the workshop was on "The translation as a manuscript," and the discussions over the four sessions were varied and lively. The problem of texts that have not been adequately edited in the source language came up for debate, as did the disturbing trend of truncating texts in translation. Other questions peculiar to the publication of translation were examined, especially the need for glossaries and footnotes. Katha's stand was delineated by Geeta Dharmarajan. Since Katha caters to a predominantly Indian readership (even expatriates, via Internet now) we do not feel the need for glossaries in our anthologies and the use of explanatory devices like footnotes is minimal. As for kinship terms, Ms Dharmarajan reiterated that Katha prefers the use of the original word from the source language as far as possible.

Most speakers emphasised the need for more creative

translations. Rajendra Yadav, the eminent writer and critic, urged translators to "look for meaning beyond lexical parallels and take into account contexts, motives and associations."

The third session of the workshop highlighted the "Anuvaad/ Roopantar" issue. Harish Trivedi detailed an interesting history of the prioritising of Anuvaad or Roopantar and held that the preference for one or other reflects the existent power equation between the source language and the target language.

As a writer whose work has been frequently translated, Nirmal Verma felt that every writer demands a different strategy from the translator and that a translator, to be truly creative, should be faithful to the spirit of the original work. These are ideas that we at Katha endorse and hope to have realised in this volume. We perceive translation as "re-vision" – a term coined by the poet Adrienne Rich, who describes it as "the act of looking back, of seeing with fresh eyes, of entering an old text from a new critical direction." As we struggle with the hundred "decisions and indecisions" that make up every act of revision, we would like to believe that we are helping in the survival of something worthwhile. Beset with these indecisions, can we expect "a final word" yet? Should we even hope for one?

June, 1995.   Meenakshi Sharma

ABOUT OUR CONTRIBUTORS

ASSAMESE

Harekrishna Deka (b 1943), a senior IPS officer of the Assam Cadre, is also a poet, short story writer and translator of poetry. He has published three collections of poems, two volumes of short stories and a book of poems in translation. *Aan Ejon*, a collection of his poems, received the Sahitya Akademi Award in 1987.

Ranjita Biswas is a freelance journalist and writer. She has translated to and from English, Assamese and Bangla. Ranjita has been an interviewer and an anchor person with AIR and Doordarshan. At present, she is a senior sub-editor with *The Telegraph*, Calcutta.

BANGLA

Lila Majumdar (b 1908) comes from an eminent literary family of West Bengal. She is one of the pioneers in the field of children's literature, having written her first story which was published in *Sandesh*, in 1922. A prolific writer of fiction and biography for children and adults, she was honoured by Government of India in 1963 for her book on Upendra Kishore Raychoudhuri.

Shampa Ghosh teaches English at SSM College in Ranchi and is currently working on her Ph. D thesis, "Symbolism in five major 19th century American novels."

Dhritiman Chatterjee was the joint winner of the award for his translation of the Bangla story.

GUJARATI

Shirish Panchal (b 1943) holds a Ph.D. from MS University, Baroda. He has published ten books. At present he edits a literary journal, *Etad*.

Madhukar Gajanan Hegde is a chemical engineer with a doctorate from the Graduate School of North Western University, Illinois. At present, he is General Manager, Nirlon Ltd. Proficient in Kannada, Marathi and Gujarati, this is his first attempt at translation.

HINDI

Mannu Bhandari (b 1931) took up writing in 1952, the year she finished her MA from Banaras Hindu University, and soon became a forerunner of the Nai Kahani Movement. With eight collections of short stories, three novels, two plays, and three novels for children, she is one of the foremost writers in Hindi today. Many of her stories have been made into very successful films and television serials.

Premila Condillac comes from a family of apple orchardists. She lives in Shimla and runs a nursery school named Roots. She has wide-ranging interests but basically sees herself as "a dabbler with no major achievements."

Ruth Vanita teaches at Miranda House, Delhi University. She is a founder member and trustee of *Manushi.* A collection of poems, *A Play of Light,* and *The Open Sky,* a translation of a novel by Rajendra Yadav have been published. Ruth shared the prize for the translation of *Nayak, Khalnayak, Vidushak* with Premila Condillac.

KANNADA

Poornachandra Tejasvi (b 1938) has written many excellent stories, several of which have been made into films. Of his two novels, the second one, *Chidambara Rahasya,* received the Sahitya Akademi Award.

Vanamala Vishwanatha teaches English in Bangalore University from where she obtained her Ph.D. Besides writing and translating to and from Kannada and English, she is a drama artiste with AIR and reads the Kannada news for Doordarshan.

KONKANI

Chandrakant Keni (b 1934) is the editor of a daily newspaper, *Rashtramat.* His short story collection, *Vhoukol Pavnni* received the Sahitya Akademi Award. The recipient of many awards from the State Academy and other institutions. He is a council member of the Sahitya Akademi and the Goa Konkani Akademi.

Vidya Pai is a freelance writer. She contributes articles and features regularly to *The Statesman*, *The Telegraph* and other periodicals.

MALAYALAM

Vaikom Muhammad Basheer (1910-1994) is one of the major influences on Malayalam literature. He introduced the "continual" story and the stream of consciousness novel to Malayalam. A versatile writer, he has written seventy-five short stories, thirteen novels, two memoirs and a play. In recognition of his considerable contribution, he was conferred a fellowship by the Sahita Akademi in 1970.

CPA Vasudevan retired as a Commissioner, Income Tax. He has contributed stories, poems, articles and book reviews to journals and newspapers. His special interest is in the field of Asian History and European expansion. A collection of his articles has been published by the International Society for the Investigation of Ancient Civilisations, Madras.

MARATHI

Vijaya Rajadhyaksha (b 1933) is an eminent writer and critic in Marathi. She has more than fifteen collections of short stories, some of which have been adapted for stage and television. A recipient of several prestigious awards, she is Head of the Post-Graduate Department of Marathi at the SNDT Women's University, Bombay.

Padmaja Punde, a journalist and a Hindustani classical vocalist, has received several scholarships for journalism and music. She performs regularly on Doordarshan and AIR and has given concerts in India and the USA. At present, she is translating a book on music from Marathi into English.

Bipin Bhise was in the Madhya Pradesh Education Service, and taught English Language and Literature at various Government colleges in the state. He enjoys reading serious fiction, watching plays and listening to classical music.

His translation of the Marathi story was selected as the joint winner of the award.

ORIYA

Jagannath Prasad Das is an art historian. He has authored two works on Orissan Art in English, eight collections of poems, five collections of short stories, five plays, a novel, poems for children, and a book of nonsense verse in Oriya.

Maurice Shukla has been teaching English and Dramatics at the Aurobindo Ashram since 1985. He translates extensively from French and Bangla. His published works include *The Lord of Horses*, a novella for children, translated from French.

PUNJABI

Ajeet Cour is a writer of fiction and a journalist with wide ranging interests. Many of her short stories have been made into films and serials for television. She has also translated and adapted outstanding literary works into Punjabi. Her contribution to Punjabi literature has been acknowledged through several honours and awards she has received including the Sahitya Akademi Award in 1986.

Jasjit Man Singh has taught in schools in India and Iran. She has authored two books, *Nanda Devi, India* and *Lt Gen Premindra Singh Bhagat, PVSM, VC: A Biography* (with Lt Gen Mathew Thomas). At present, she is a freelance copy editor.

Devinder Kaur Assa Singh obtained a doctorate in Psychology from London University in 1933. She and her sisters started the Bhai Bishen Singh Satsangi Trust to support the education of girls in rural India. Her interests are reading and alternative medicine.

TAMIL

Na Muthuswamy (b 1936) comes from Punjai, a village near the mouth of the Kaveri. He trains actors at Koothu-p-pattarai, a full time experimental theatre group and his recent short stories have been specially written to train his actors in speech.

Shakuntala Ramani has been closely associated with Kalakshetra, Madras. She is the chairperson of the Craft Education and Research Centre, and a member of its Academic Committee. She edited the arts and crafts magazine, *Nunkalai*. At present she is on the advisory board of the Tamil Nadu Lalit Kala Akademi.

URDU

Surendra Prakash is one of the first few writers of the new short story in Urdu, which had its origins in the fifties. His collection of short stories, *Baz Goyi* is considered a milestone in Urdu literature. He now writes scripts for films and television serials.

Sara Rai is a writer and translator with a number of publications to her credit. She has translated and edited a collection of stories from Hindi, *The Golden Waist Chain and Other Stories*. She manages the Munshi Premchand Memorial School, Allahabad, and is writing a book and working on some translations.

ABOUT KATHA

KATHA is a registered nonprofit organisation devoted to creative communication for development. Katha's basic objective is to spread the love of books and the joy of reading amongst children and adults. Our activities span from literacy to literature.

KALPAVRIKSHAM, Katha's Centre for Sustainable Learning, develops and publishes quality material for neo-literate children and adults, and works with teachers to help them make their teaching and presentation more creative. The publications for first-generation schoolgoers and adult neo-literates are learning packages, specially designed for use in nonformal education — *Hulgul Ka Pitara* a basic Hindi language package, *Anmol Khazana*, a kit on sustainable living and *Chaand!*, an integrated kit for the teaching of science, maths and language. And there is *Tamasha!* a fun and activity magazine on development issues for children in Hindi and English. The *Katha Vachak* books and monthly tabloid are for the reading pleasure of neo-literates, especially women.

THE KHAZANA EXPERIMENT, a part of Kalpavriksham, is a project in Delhi's largest slum cluster at Govindpuri, started in 1990. This "deschool" and income generation programme caters to almost 1200 working children and about 100 women.

The proceeds from the sale of Katha's various publications go to support this project.

KATHA VILASAM is the Story Research And Resource Centre of Katha. It seeks to foster and applaud the best short fiction from the regional languages and take it to a wider readership through translations. The Katha Awards, instituted in1990, are given annually to the best short fiction published in the regional languages that year, and for translations of these stories. Through projects like the Translation Contest it attempts to build up a bank of sensitive translators. In addition to this, Katha Vilasam functions as a literary agency and works with academia to associate students in translation-related activities. KathaNet, an invaluable network of Friends of Katha, is the mainstay of all Katha Vilasam efforts.

WHAT THEY SAY...

Katha Prize Stories Series

1991

Fastidiously hand-picked with an accent on the inherent heterogeneity and cultural complexity of contemporary India ...   *–Sunday Chronicle*

... an excellent collection ... the range of craftsmanship and technique is amazing ...   *–The Hindu*

1992

... a publishing feat ... The stories ... have the earthy vitality of a live language and the advantages of a refined narrative technique.
                                        –The Daily

1993

... the pioneering effort to bring out translated versions ... moistens the barren patch of short fiction in English ... near flawless end-products.
                                        –Indian Express

A fundamental collection.   *–The Book Review*

... an anxiously awaited yearly event watched alike by discerning readers in India and abroad as well as by writers, translators and literary journals.
                                        —The Economic Times

1994

The fare is rich and diverse ...   *–Business Standard*

Translation is the essence of national integration. The discovery of the wealth of Indian creative writing through translation is an inspiration. Katha is a part of this discovery.   *– India Today*

Katha Regional Fiction: *A Southern Harvest*
... an eye opener   *–Business Standard*

Tamasha! the only fun and activity magazine for children on development issues

Children love *Tamasha!* because
- it has exciting stories
- unusual and interesting facts
- innovative games and puzzles
- imaginative illustrations that reach out to you from every page

'... from general knowledge to games, ecology to education and health, every subject is treated with the right balance of information and diversion ...'
> – Sakuntala Narasimhan in Sunday Herald

'... with extremely attractive pictures, *Tamasha!* is sure to make an impact on the child reader ... Definitely a must for those who are in the field of rural communication ...'
> – Vijaya Ghose in Book Review

'... very educative, creative.'
> – WAF Hopper, The Church of South India, Council for Education

'An excellent publication: imaginative, attractive and useful.'
> – J Peter Greaves, UNICEF, New York, USA.

A magazine for every well-informed child

KATHA

in association with
the British High Commission,
British Council Division,
announces

**The Second
All India Translation Contest, 1995-96.**

Another opportunity for you to translate
great short fiction from twelve regional
languages into English

Prize winning translations will be published
by Katha in its Regional Fiction Series

For more information write to
KATHA
PO Box 326
New Delhi 110 001
Please enclose a stamped self-addressed
envelope